BACK
TO ME

Earl Sewell

BACK
TO ME

HARLEQUIN®

entertain, enrich, inspire™

Recycling programs
for this product may
not exist in your area.

BACK TO ME

ISBN-13: 978-0-373-53466-1

www.Harlequin.com

Printed in U.S.A.

Acknowledgments

I want to say thank you to the following people for all their help with my endless questions.

To my editor, Glenda Howard, who has stood with me and who has been a champion of my career and this new series from the beginning. Thank you so much for your belief in my work and talent.

I have to send out an extra-special thank-you to Dr. Marcia Brevard Wynn. Thank you for all the encouragement and guidance you've given me. Your philosophy and thought-provoking insights on life and happiness have inspired me beyond words. You're truly one of a kind, but I'm certain you already know that.

To Lauren Wynn, for taking the time out of your busy social schedule to read every teen book I've written and provide me with your feedback, comments and suggestions. They were truly helpful.

To Taryn Kingery, librarian, the Ralph Ellison Library, Oklahoma City, Megan Murray Cusick, Nancy B. Jefferson Alternative School. Thank you both for sharing my work and for encouraging young people to read. The world truly needs more people like you.

To my daughter Candice, I love you more than words can express. And to Ms. Jan Washington, thanks for the great brownie recipe.

To all who have discovered my teen titles and have either shared them with or recommended them to young readers, thank you so much for helping me spread the word.

Please feel free to drop me a line at earl@earlsewell.com. Please put the title of my book in the subject line so that I know your message is not spam. Make sure you check out www.earlsewell.net and www.myspace.com/earlsewell. You can also hit me up on Facebook and Twitter. Just type in my name and you should be able to find me with little difficulty.

"Revenge only engenders violence, not clarity and true peace.
I think liberation must come from within."
—Sandra Cisneros

one

VIVIANA

My cousin Anna had the height and the natural stride of a model. She was slimmer than most girls, and if you asked me, she had the beauty and personality that could land her on the covers of magazines. Anna and I were goofing around. She was trying on various outfits and pretending to walk a runway like Tyra Banks and Adriana Lima. I was playing music for her as she strutted back and forth. Anna then asked me to join her private fashion show, but neither one of us could stop laughing long enough to walk from one end of the bedroom to the other. We decided to have more fun by dancing. Anna set up her webcam so we could post videos of our foolishness on YouTube and some popular social networks. What I didn't realize was that in addition to being very pretty, Anna could dance. If I were her manager, I'd enter her in a reality television dance contest. Seriously, she had some moves that left my mouth wide open.

"Oh, girl. You are tripping. You should be getting paid for dancing the way you do," I said, feeling envious of how well she moved.

"I'm just flexible, that's all," Anna said as she got up and moved toward her dresser drawer.

"Didn't you used to take dance lessons when you were little?" I asked, vaguely recalling hearing Grandmother Esmeralda praising one of her performances.

"That was years ago, when I was a little girl. Mom had me in ballet class and modeling classes. I wasn't very good at ballet, so I tried modern dance, which was more fun. All of the dancing made me look more muscular, which my modeling coach at the time said was unacceptable. I stopped doing that stuff when I was around eleven."

"Why did you stop?" I was curious.

"I was forced to choose between dancing and modeling, and I couldn't, because I enjoyed both equally," said Anna as she removed a purple belly dancer's hip scarf from the top dresser drawer.

"What the heck is this?" I said louder than I intended to as I reached out to touch the silky fabric.

"Mom and I took a beginner's belly dance class last year," Anna explained. "It was only four classes, but I learned a lot and it was fun."

Anna tied the scarf around her hips. She looked very cute in it. She reset her webcam, put on song by Shakira called "Hips Don't Lie," and right before my eyes she began working her hips just like the singer. She rocked those bad boys like a belly dancer, and the movements she did with her torso were nothing short of mesmerizing. About the only thing I could really do well was make my booty bounce. When Anna was done, she posted her video for the world to see.

"You have to teach me how to dance like that." I was practically begging her.

"Sure. It's really easy, and I'm sure you can make it look far sexier than I can," Anna said.

"You're doing it in the sexy dancing department if you ask me." I chuckled.

"Then why was Carlo more interested in Maya than me?" she asked.

"Because he was stupid, and the last thing you want is a stupid boyfriend," I assured her.

Anna laughed. "You're right. Come stand next to me and I'll show you how to do some hip snaps."

"Hip snaps?" I asked, because it sounded painful.

"Yes, like this." Anna demonstrated the move, and the coins on her hip scarf shimmied and jingled.

"That move is so hot," I said as I moved closer to her and tried. I knew I looked silly, because my hips wouldn't snap the way Anna's had.

"No. You have to bend your knees like this, tuck your pelvis forward, squeeze your butt and then shift from one hip to the other," Anna instructed.

I did the move right twice but felt as if something got dislocated. "Oh, my God. I think I broke my hip," I said.

"No, you didn't. Your body is just not used to moving in that way," she said and encouraged me to keep trying. Anna and I were having a blast dancing, posting videos and being obnoxious. We were in the middle of dancing when Anna's older sister, Maya, entered the room unannounced.

"It's one-thirty in the morning. Why are you guys up so late?" Maya asked.

"We're having a party and you're not invited," Anna said.

"I wouldn't party with your bony behind, anyway." I could tell right away that Maya had caught an immediate attitude.

Anna shook her hips and rattled the coins in Maya's direction as a sign of defiance.

"You know, Anna, for someone who almost died recently, don't you think you're overdoing it a bit?" Maya asked.

"No, she isn't," I said. "She is only showing me how to dance, Maya. Do you have a problem with that?" I asked.

"I have a problem with everything. Especially you, Viviana." Maya was kick-starting some drama.

I was happy that Anna was back home from the hospital and doing well. I still couldn't believe she'd accidentally ingested crystal meth. Seeing her lying in a hospital bed with tubes and needles connected to her arms wasn't a nice experience. I thought for sure she was going to die and I'd get blamed for it. I was just so glad that didn't happen. Besides, I didn't know what I'd do if my favorite cousin wasn't around. I loved my cousin Anna but totally hated her sister, Maya. Anna was so much easier to get along with. She didn't judge me or treat me as if I was beneath her the way Maya did.

"Don't come in here taking out your anger on us because Misalo has dumped you," I snapped back at her. I wasn't about to let her nasty comment go unanswered.

"I'm not taking anything out on you guys. All I'm asking is for you to be quieter. I'm trying to get some rest." Maya tried to come off as if she wasn't trying to be confrontational, but I knew better.

"Anna, you don't have to listen to her. We are not being loud," I said.

Maya decided to play dirty. "Do you guys want me to get Mom involved? Because I can."

"Fine, Maya. We'll keep it down." Anna gave in to her sister.

"Thank you," Maya said and paused briefly. "By the way, it is good to see you up and moving around again," she said as she exited the room and shut the door.

"That girl needs to get a life," I grumbled. "I don't see how you can stand living with her."

"Maya is just Maya. She always feels like she has to be the mature one," Anna explained.

"Well, she should try being a kid sometimes. I mean, seriously. She could've come in here and asked if she could join us and had fun being silly," I said.

"That's not Maya," Anna said as she selected another song for us to dance to. She turned down the volume and began shimmying her hips again when the music began. I watched as Anna lost herself in the rhythm of the music.

"Come on. Stop pouting and dance with me," Anna said, snapping me out of my daydream.

I smiled, rose to my feet and joined her.

The following morning I was sitting at the kitchen table, eating breakfast with Aunt Raven, Maya and Anna. Uncle Herman was at a friend's house, helping out with some type of home-improvement project. I was enjoying the buttermilk pancakes, scrambled eggs, sausage links and hash browns Aunt Raven had prepared. I really didn't have anything exciting planned for my day, with the exception of just hanging out and doing whatever. Living in the suburbs was so much different than living in the city. The suburbs were totally boring. I just didn't see how people functioned when there was absolutely nothing going on. At least in the city there was always something to enjoy—a block party, a festival or a barbecue—and if nothing like that was going on, you could always just hang out on the street, where it was guaranteed that something would come up. Heck, out here I couldn't even get away and walk along the lakefront, something I enjoyed doing when I was staying with my mom and her trifling boyfriend.

"So, Viviana, how well were you doing in school?" asked Aunt Raven. The question came out of nowhere and caused me to stop chewing my food and glare at her.

"What do you mean?" I asked as I swallowed my food. I wasn't sure what she wanted to know.

"Well, you and Maya are the same age. What high school were you attending?" she asked, rephrasing her question.

"Why?" I didn't understand why she even cared to know that information.

"Well, you've been staying with us for a few weeks, and since it looks like you'll be staying here for a while longer, I have to see what I can do about getting you registered at Thornwood. You may luck out and get to take some classes with Maya," she said. Obviously, Maya and I were hiding our disdain for each other very well.

"Can we talk about this later? School is a rather touchy subject for me," I said, wanting her to drop the conversation.

"No. I feel that this is an appropriate time to discuss this. You have nothing to be ashamed of," she assured me.

At that moment, I wanted to push away from the table and storm out of the room, but I knew that wouldn't go over very well with my aunt.

"Seriously, can't we just talk about this issue later?" I tried pleading with her in hopes she'd catch my drift.

"What is wrong with you, Viviana? It's just a simple question," my aunt said, pressing the issue.

"Yeah, Viviana. I'd also like to know what school you went to," Maya interjected. "Were you on the cheerleading squad? No. Scratch that question. You don't look like the cheerleading type. Maybe you were on the school dance team? You seem to know how to dance like a—"

Aunt Raven cut her off before she finished. "Maya!"

"What? I was going to say like a trained professional," Maya smirked. I could tell from her condescending grin that her comment was loaded with sarcasm.

"Now, Viviana, what's the name of the school where you were last registered?" Aunt Raven wasn't going to let our conversation rest. I really didn't want to tell her, because I was carrying a secret I was certain she'd find inexcusable.

"Roberto Clemente," I answered, not wanting to offer any more information than necessary.

"So, you should've finished your junior year, right?" My aunt had asked the question that I had hoped she wouldn't. I stopped eating my food and exhaled loudly. I shot my eyes over at Maya, who was glaring at me as if she were trying to read my thoughts. When I didn't answer, she made her own assumptions.

"OMG," Maya blurted out.

Startled, Aunt Raven asked, "What?"

"Mom, isn't it obvious? She didn't finish her junior year." Miss Know-It-All Maya Rogers pointed her shameful finger at me. I wanted to rip it off and shove it up her nose until it came out of her eye socket.

"You shouldn't talk about things you don't know about!" I snapped.

"Wait a minute. There is no need to argue or get nasty with each other. Viviana Anita Vargas, is what Maya said true?" My aunt had called me by my full name. I took my eyes off of Maya and cut them over to Aunt Raven.

"No," I answered her.

"Good. I'll look up the address of the school and request a copy of your transcript. I'll have to figure out how I'll explain to them that I'm your current guardian."

"I haven't been there in a long time. They probably don't have it anymore," I said, hoping that the administrators and teachers had completely forgotten about me.

"It's because you've been on summer vacation, right?" asked Anna.

I glanced at her briefly before lowering my eyes with humility. Embarrassment began swelling in my heart like the sun rising in the morning. I felt as if I were being judged.

"Viviana, hold your head up and stop slouching. There is no need to look as if someone has beaten the life out of you," said Aunt Raven.

"I didn't attend school for most of my junior year. I

haven't earned the credits needed to pass, okay? Are you guys happy now? I said it!" It was very hard for me to admit that. It was an awful burden weighing on my heart.

"That explains a lot," Maya remarked and snickered.

My humiliation immediately evaporated. I wanted to reach across the table and scratch up her face like a dog digging a hole in the backyard. I slammed my hand against the table and rose to my feet. I was ready to leap across the table and kick her butt for making me feel like crap. "I've got more smarts than you'll ever know about, Maya!" I barked at her.

"Hey, hey, hey!" Aunt Raven wasn't about to let my hostility go unchecked. "There is absolutely no need for that. Maya apologize to her."

"What for?" she asked.

"For being so insensitive."

"You're kidding, right?" Maya looked as if she'd just been asked to pick up dog crap with her bare hands.

"No, I'm not."

Reluctantly, Maya mumbled, "Sorry."

Aunt Raven released a deep sigh as she pinched the bridge of her nose with her thumb and forefinger. "Okay. So, you haven't been in school for a while. How did that happen?" she asked.

Shrugging my shoulders, I said, "It just did. Mom was always moving. She'd pack our things at the drop of a dime and move on. It didn't matter if I was in the middle of the school year or not."

Aunt Raven focused on me and remained silent for a long moment. It was as if she wanted to say something but didn't know exactly how to phrase her words.

"It's not that serious," I snapped. I wanted to disappear. I reasoned with myself that it would be best for me to go back to the city and do my own thing. I didn't need or want their pity. I hustled toward the back door that led out to the driveway. I was more than willing to hitch-hike all the way back to Chicago, to Grandmother Es-meralda's house.

"Viviana!" I heard Aunt Raven call my name, but I ignored her.

Just as I was about to sprint down the driveway, I saw an old, brown, rusted-out Chevy pickup truck pulling in.

"Who in the hell is this?" I heard Aunt Raven ask from behind me.

"I have no idea," I said, trying to make out the face of the driver. It was difficult to do because of the sun's glare reflecting off the windshield.

"They must be lost or something," said Aunt Raven as she walked toward the vehicle.

The car came to a halt, and the passenger door swung open. I was in total shock when I saw my mom step out of the truck. I rushed toward her, happy to see that she was okay. I wrapped my arms around her, not caring about the stench of cigar smoke that had saturated her clothing. I stepped out of our embrace to look at her once more. She was wearing a burgundy top with white capri pants that were see-through. I could see the pink-and-white-striped underwear she had on. It was without question a major fashion mistake, even I knew, but my mother probably thought it made her look sexy.

"It's so good to see you, Mom. I've missed you," I admitted, embracing her again and holding on to her even tighter.

"I've missed you, Vivi," my mother said, calling me by the nickname she'd given me.

Not wanting to let go of her, I said, "I want to go with you."

Ignoring my comment, she said, "Look at you, Viviana, living all fancy with your cousins." She admired Aunt Raven's house as if she were visiting for the first time.

"Will we ever get a house like this?" I asked, hoping she'd somehow been able to do better.

"Someday, baby. You, me and Martin will be a happy family, living in a big, fancy house. One even better than this one," she said, detaching herself from my embrace as she continued looking around the property.

"Well, for your sake, I would hope that someday is pretty soon." Aunt Raven gave my mom a brief hug.

"Do you have anything to eat? Martin and I are starving," my mother said.

"Martin? Who is Martin?" asked Aunt Raven.

"The love of my life." My mom turned back to the truck and waved for Martin to step out.

"How is everybody doing?" Martin asked as he got out of the truck. As he walked around to where we were, he had to jack his pants up in order to cover his butt crack.

"Ew-wee," I mumbled as he approached.

My mom introduced them. "Raven, this is Martin. Martin, this is my sister, Raven."

"Nice to meet you." Aunt Raven greeted him with a handshake.

I glanced at Martin, noticing his bad eye, and had to

immediately look away out of fear I'd go cross-eyed if I stared at him too long.

"Is it all right if I leave the truck parked right here?" Martin asked.

"Sure. It's not a problem," Aunt Raven answered.

"So, are you going to invite us in?" my mom asked.

"Yeah, sure. We were just finishing breakfast," Aunt Raven said. As we walked back toward the house, Martin noticed the gas barbecue grill.

"See, baby. That's the kind of grill I want to get once we find a place to settle down. You know how important my food is to me, and I'll barbecue at the drop of a hat," Martin said jokingly.

"I can't wait for that day, baby," said my mom. The fact that she was still with Martin made my stomach flip.

When we walked back inside, Maya and Anna had cleared the table and placed the dishes in the dishwasher. I assumed they had gone back to their rooms and didn't realize that my mom and Martin had arrived. We made our way to the family room.

"This is a real nice place you've got here," Martin said, admiring the decor.

"Thank you. Why don't you have a seat?" Aunt Raven said as she grabbed the remote control for the television. She turned it on for him and quickly showed him how to change the channels. "Would you like something to drink?" Aunt Raven offered.

"A beer would be great," said Martin as he got immediately comfortable.

"It's still very early in the morning, and you're driving,"

Aunt Raven pointed out. I guess she thought it would make a difference to Martin.

"Honey, I can drink tequila and ride a motorcycle backward with my eyes closed. A beer isn't going to do much to me."

I could tell by the way Aunt Raven threaded her eyebrows together that she didn't like what he'd just said. "I'm sorry. I don't have any beer or tequila."

"Don't worry about it, baby. I'm sure I'll find something for you. My sister always keeps something around the house," said my mom, who was once again bending over backward to accommodate this jerk's every wish.

"Salena, we need to talk," I heard Aunt Raven say.

"Yes, we do," my mother agreed, as if nothing about the situation seemed awkward. We went back upstairs and into the kitchen. I sat back down at the table with my mother and Aunt Raven.

"Isn't Martin wonderful?" my mom asked, glowing as if she were truly in love.

"I don't know. I haven't really gotten to know the man, but first impressions make me think he has an alcoholism issue."

"There you go already, Raven. You're about to start with the crap!" My mom had gotten offended.

"What? I've never been around the type of man who drinks tequila and rides a motorcycle backward. Is he a stuntman or something?" asked Aunt Raven.

"He's a good man, and that's all that matters," my mother replied, defending her relationship with Martin.

"Mom, where have you been?" I asked.

"Yes. Why did you abandon your daughter?" Aunt Raven added.

"What the hell are you talking about, Raven? I didn't abandon her. I left her with Mom."

"You know our mother has health issues and can't take care of Viviana." I could tell by the pitch of Aunt Raven's voice that she was getting irritated.

"Don't let that old woman fool you. She's not as sickly as she pretends to be. I know that for a fact," said my mom. "Besides, I'm back for her now."

"Really? Do you have a place for us to live?" I asked, even though the thought of Martin living with us was creepy.

"Well, not exactly. Martin wants to drive back to his hometown in Louisiana. He said that we can get a mobile home at a really reasonable price. Once he finds work, that's where we'll live," she said.

"Where will you stay until he finds a job?" Aunt Raven asked.

"We'll stay at a hotel or sleep in the truck." My mom spoke as if nothing was abnormal about that.

My aunt raised her voice disapprovingly. "How are the three of you going to sleep in a pickup truck?"

"Oh, it's not so bad. We'll just treat it like we're on a camping trip," said my mom.

"Have you lost your mind?" Aunt Raven shrieked.

"Hey! I'm doing the best that I can, okay!" my mom yelled.

"Maybe it won't be that bad," I said, trying to show support for my mom, but in my heart I knew I could not make it sleeping in a pickup truck. I'm a tough Latina, but not that resilient.

"My God, Salena. I swear, sometimes I have a hard time believing you're my sister," said Aunt Raven as she combed her fingers through her hair.

"Everyone isn't perfect like you, Raven. Mom and Dad loved you more. I never got all the things or the attention you got. You could never do wrong in their eyes!"

"Why are you bringing up something that doesn't even matter in this situation? I'm talking about providing a stable home for your daughter, and you're bringing up crap from thirty years ago," Aunt Raven snapped.

"Because it is important, and you know it. Had I gotten just a little bit of the encouragement that you received, I'd be a better woman today."

"No. You're the woman you are today because of the choices you've made." Aunt Raven's words made perfect sense to me, but my mother just didn't want to hear the naked truth. Instead she twisted it into something she could use.

"Choices," said my mom and then paused. "You're right. We all have choices to make. If you think I'm such a horrible mother, what choice are you going to make to fix or help me change my situation?"

Exhaling loudly, Aunt Raven said, "Look, maybe I can talk to Herman, and you and Viviana could stay with us until you're able to find a job and get on your feet, but I know Herman isn't going to let Martin live here. I wouldn't dare ask him to agree to that."

"Yeah, Mom, I like that idea," I chimed in, agreeing with the solution Aunt Raven was offering.

"Hell no!" My mother flat out refused the offer. "I wouldn't go back to living under the same roof with you if I were blind, crippled and crazy."

"You can't live out of a damn pickup truck, Salena!" Aunt Raven barked.

"You can't tell me what I can and can't do! See, that's your freaking problem, Raven. You're too damn bossy."

Aunt Raven tossed her hands up. "I'm done. Talking common sense to you is pointless."

"So, you don't want me living in the pickup truck, right?" my mother asked.

"No," answered Aunt Raven as she removed a glass from the cupboard. She filled it with crushed ice from the refrigerator, then with water. "Your lifestyle isn't of concern to me. I am worried about Viviana, though."

"Okay, then help me out, for Viviana's sake," my mom said.

"I'm trying to. Lord knows that I am," answered Aunt Raven.

"Help me out by giving me a loan," my mother said.

"You still owe me two thousand dollars, Salena. I'm not giving you any more money," Aunt Raven said.

"That's not a lot of money for you." My mother didn't give much weight to being in debt to her sister.

Aunt Raven took a drink of water and then just stared into her glass. There was a long moment of silence.

"Get your things, Viviana. We're not welcome here," said my mother.

"Viviana isn't going anywhere. And for the record, I never said that she wasn't welcome here," Aunt Raven said.

"No. Viviana is coming with me and Martin to Louisiana," my mother insisted.

"Viviana needs to go to school," Aunt Raven said. "And she can't do that with a registered address being a pickup truck."

"She can worry about school later," said my mom.

"Salena, do you even understand what you're saying?" asked Aunt Raven.

"What? Are you trying to say that I don't take good care of her?" My mother growled her words like a lion.

"No, you don't. You've moved around so much that Viviana hasn't earned enough credits to move into her senior year of high school. If you keep moving around like this, she's going to end up being kicked out of high school because she'll age out of the system. A seventeen-year-old sophomore isn't acceptable. She needs stability. She needs a place to call home."

"If she gets kicked out, she can take the GED test. It's not a big deal." My mother pointed her index finger at Aunt Raven.

"Don't put your finger in my face," Aunt Raven warned her.

There was another moment of silence. Finally, Aunt Raven spoke. "Viviana, you should go upstairs."

"Why?" I asked, not wanting to leave. I looked at my mother to see if I should excuse myself or stay put.

"Run along, Viviana," my mom said. "Raven and I need to work this out."

"You're not going to get into a fistfight, are you?" I asked.

"No," they both said simultaneously.

"Okay, I just wanted to make sure," I said, getting up from the table. As I made my way back upstairs, I saw Aunt Raven pick up her cell phone. I paused for a moment to see who she was calling. I eavesdropped on the conversation.

"Hello, Mom. It's me, Raven. Salena has surfaced," I heard her say.

TWO

After watching Viviana rush out of the house like a two-year-old having a temper tantrum, I went up to my bedroom. I couldn't believe she had missed most of her junior year of high school and had to repeat it. I know it wasn't totally her fault, but it still didn't stop me from thinking she wasn't all that bright of a student. I also wasn't feeling the idea of my mom wanting to let her stay. I wanted Viviana to leave. The longer she stayed around, the more I got a bad feeling something crazy was going to jump off.

I closed my door and grabbed my cell phone from the nightstand, where it was recharging. I saw that I'd received several text messages, and hoped at least one of them was from Misalo. When I checked, I found that there were several photos of shirtless male friends I knew. I shouldn't really call them friends, since they were just guys from the neighborhood that both Misalo and I hung out with. One shirtless photo had a message that read, Maya, I didn't know you were so freaky. Heard you broke up with Misalo. Hit me back, Bobby.

There was also a photo of Hector, wearing only his

boxer shorts. In the photo he was trying to flex his scrawny biceps muscle, which had a tattoo of a skull. His message read, I can give you all of this and a lot more. Misalo was stupid for letting a super freak like you go. Come see what it feels like to be with a real man, baby. The final one was from a boy named Bailey, who was on the soccer team with Misalo. He forwarded a photo of his pierced tongue. His message read, I have front row tickets to the Lil Wayne concert. What are you willing to do for them? Frustrated and ticked off that they were doing this, I shot them all text messages back that read, Oh, hell to the no! I wouldn't date you if you were the last idiot on the planet! Now leave me alone!

I heard a knock at my door. "Go away!" I said. Whoever was there clearly didn't understand English, because I saw the door creep open. "Hey, I said get the hell—" I didn't finish, because I saw that it was my best friend, Keysha. She was wearing blue jean shorts, a white tank top and some cute sandals. She also had a cute pink scarf covering her damp hair. Keysha worked part-time as a lifeguard at the pool, and liked to cover her hair at the end of her shift.

"I didn't tell you to enter," I said condescendingly.

"Whoa, where is this hostility coming from? I came over here to see how you were doing," Keysha said defensively.

"I'm sorry," I apologized. "I'm just in a really funky mood."

Keysha came in and closed the door. "I think your mom is talking to her sister. And did you know that Viviana is blocking the steps, looking like she has to send a late text to her boyfriend?" she asked.

"Huh?" I was completely confused by what Keysha was saying.

Chuckling, Keysha said, "It's something I overheard. Some guys were at the pool, boasting about how many girls they'd slept with. One of them said, 'I love having sex, so I use latex so that my girl won't send me a late text.' It was the dumbest thing I'd ever heard, but Viviana has a look on her face like she needs to send a late text."

"Please! That chick couldn't get the ugliest boy on the planet to even look in her direction. Her attitude is nastier than a baboon's behind."

"Wow," Keysha said, surprised by my total dislike of Viviana.

"I'll run down and see my aunt Salena later," I said as I sat down at the foot of my bed. I released a long, depressing sigh. Keysha came and sat next to me. She draped her arm around me and gave me a big hug. I leaned forward and placed my face in the palms of my hands. I gave myself permission to cry while Keysha rocked me.

"Come on, girl. If you start crying, then I'll start, too," Keysha said.

I got a lasso around my emotions before getting up to pull a few Kleenex tissues from a box on top of my dresser.

"Have you heard from him?" Keysha asked.

"No. He won't return my phone calls," I said.

"Maybe he'll answer if I call," Keysha said.

"Would you?" I asked, feeling as if Misalo might answer her phone call.

"Yeah," Keysha said. She removed her cell phone from her pocket and called him. She then handed me the phone. After several rings, Misalo answered the phone.

"Hey, honey," I said as sweetly as I could.

"Keysha? I know you're not trying to hook up with me," Misalo said.

"This isn't Keysha," I said innocently. "It's me, Maya. Can we talk?" I asked.

"Maya, I'm not going to play these games with you. Obviously you've been secretly dealing with Carlo behind my back. I just wish you could have owned up to the fact that you wanted someone else. You didn't have to string me along, as if we had something special that couldn't be broken."

"We do have something special. This is all just a big misunderstanding, baby," I said, hoping my honey-coated words would reach his heart.

"Maya, you were slow dancing with another guy at a party. I'm done with you," he said with absolute certainty.

"But I'm not ready for you to be done with me," I said, feeling my tears swell.

"You should've thought about that before you started creeping with Carlo," Misalo replied, raising his voice at me.

Raising my voice back, I asked, "Will you at least give me a chance to explain my side of the story?"

"Maya, I don't…" He paused. "You know what? You're not the woman I thought you were. Just stop bothering me," he said and hung up. I felt as numb as a rock as I sat there with the phone to my ear, as if he would return and say he was sorry. I felt as if the world had stopped time. I couldn't bring myself to believe that it was over between Misalo and me.

"What did he say?" asked Keysha.

"He hates me," I whispered as more tears fell from my eyes.

Keysha attempted to make me feel better. "He doesn't hate you. Misalo loves you."

"I have to do something. I'm not going to let this happen," I said, suddenly feeling angry.

"What are you going to do?" Keysha asked.

"I don't know, but I'm not giving up. I'll fight for him if I have to," I said with absolute resolve.

"Well, you know I'm here for you," Keysha said, offering her support.

Smearing away my tears of sadness, I turned to her and said, "I love him, Keysha. If his heart is broken, then so is mine. If he feels sad, then so do I. When his soul is wounded, so is mine. He knows in his heart that I wasn't trying to hurt him."

"Okay, let's go back a little. Tell me again what happened," Keysha said.

"I'm telling you, it was nothing. I snuck out of the house," I explained.

"I still can't believe you did that," Keysha remarked.

"I know. I'm so perfect, right? I never do anything wild or crazy. I'm always the responsible one," I said mockingly.

"But that's who you are. As long as I've known you, you've never pulled the sneak-out-of-the-house stunt." Keysha reminded me of my untarnished record.

"Have you forgotten about the party I went to where I got my leg broken?" I reminded her.

"No, but that was different," Keysha said.

"How? It was a party that I wasn't supposed to be at," I said, stating the facts.

"Okay, fair enough. So maybe you're not as perfect as I'm making you out to be, but you're certainly not a wild child." Keysha moved over to my bedroom window and glanced out of it. "Looks like your aunt is leaving," she said.

"Really! Is she taking Viviana with her?" I asked as I sprang to my feet to glance out the window. I saw my aunt and this hulking guy get into a hideous pickup truck. "Eww! What a crappy-looking car," I said.

"I know. As I came up the driveway, I peeked inside, and, man, was it junky in there. Dude seriously needs to clean out his ride," Keysha mentioned.

I grumbled as I saw the pickup truck back out of the driveway. "They didn't take Viviana."

"Wow. How much longer is she going to be here?" Keysha asked.

"I have no clue," I said. "One thing is for sure. I'm never going to trust her again."

"I wouldn't, either, especially after she left you stranded the way she did." Keysha pointed out the fact that Viviana had attended the party with me and then had left me stranded.

"Anyway, if I hadn't run into Carlo at the party, I don't know how I would've gotten back home."

Keysha cleared her throat and said, "Excuse me. I was

on the phone with you that night, offering to pay for your cab fare home."

"I know, Keysha. Thank you for being there for me," I said earnestly.

"You're lucky you're my BFF, because I wouldn't shell out money like that for anyone else," she said.

"I can't wait to get my driver's license," I said.

Keysha snapped her fingers. "I forgot to tell you," she said excitedly.

"Tell me what?" I asked.

Keysha stood in the center of my bedroom and started doing her happy dance. "My dad has signed me up for private driving lessons. I'm going to be getting my permit and then my driver's license. Then bam! He's going to buy me a car. And when that happens, girl, we are going to be driving all over town."

"Why didn't you remind me to ask my dad so that we could take the class together?"

"Because on the day I was going to tell you, all of the drama with Misalo happened." Keysha stopped dancing around.

I sighed. "Do you think I should buy him something? It would be my way of asking for a truce."

Keysha shrugged her shoulders. "It couldn't hurt. Maybe if he sees how sorry you truly are, he'll give you another chance. Still, in my honest opinion, I think Misalo is overreacting to this entire situation."

"I think so, too." I felt a swell of sadness rising in my heart once again. "Keysha, I want you to be totally honest with me," I said.

"I always am," Keysha reminded me.

"If Wesley, Antonio or Jerry were to come back, saying they were sorry for what they did, which one would you give another chance to?" I asked.

"Wow," Keysha said as she pondered that one. "In all honesty, the only one I'd truly believe was sorry would be Wesley."

"So, you're saying you'd give him another chance?" I asked, just to be extra sure.

Keysha banged the heel of her hand against the side of her head a few times.

"Why are you hitting yourself like that?" I asked, completely confused.

"My scalp itches. The water at the pool has really made my hair dry. Plus, it's about time for these braids to come out."

"Okay. You need to warn me before you do that again. I thought you were freaking out or something." I chuckled.

"Ha-ha," she said.

"So, answer my question," I insisted.

"If the circumstances were right, I'd go back to Wesley," Keysha said.

"Wow! Really?" I asked, thinking for sure she'd give Jerry another shot.

"Yeah. There is just something about Wesley that is kind of pure and innocent," Keysha explained. "So, what are we going to do? I have the day off."

"I don't know. Maybe you should just go and do your own thing today. I'm sort of in a really jacked-up mood," I said truthfully.

"Well, that's what best friends are for. We pull each

other out of the dumps. You know the Heritage Summer Festival is going on today at the park. We could put on some cute outfits and go see if some hot guys will be there."

"I don't feel like changing clothes. I just want to sit around and mope."

"You could go there and shop for a nice, unique gift for Misalo. Besides, I wouldn't be surprised if he was there. I overheard lots of people at the pool talking about going." Keysha knew exactly what to say to get me motivated.

Perking up, I said, "Yeah, you're probably right." I moved over to my closet and opened it. "Come on, Keysha. Help me find something to wear."

"That's the spirit, girl! Sitting in a room, all gloomy, thinking about what happened will drive you crazy. On top of that, crazy doesn't look good on you."

"I agree, but it's not easy getting over a broken heart," I admitted as another wave of depression wrapped around me like a warm blanket.

Three

VIVIANA

I didn't go up to Anna's room as Aunt Raven had asked me to. Instead, I walked up a few steps, situated myself so I couldn't be seen, then leaned over the banister, eavesdropping on the conversation my mother and aunt were having with Grandmother Esmeralda. I was able to hear my mother say, "What do you want from me? You want me to admit that I'm not as good as Raven?" I could tell by her tone of voice that my mother was on the brink of having another one of her classic "Get off my back" episodes. I was trying to listen in so hard that I got startled when I saw Maya's friend Keysha coming up the stairs.

"Excuse me," she said as if she was royalty and I was some annoying peasant.

"Do you have a problem with saying hello first?" I asked.

Keysha snickered at me. "I am not the one," she said, stepping past me.

I flipped up my middle finger behind her back before leaning back over the banister to eavesdrop again. I couldn't hear very much, so I just stood there, wondering what would happen next.

Eventually, my mom came looking for me. When she saw me standing on the stairs, she asked me to come take a walk with her. We went out into the backyard and stood under the shade of a tree.

"Look, you're going to have to stay with your aunt Raven a little while longer," she began explaining.

"Are you leaving me again?" My voice was edgy.

"It's not so bad here," my mother said defensively.

"I don't want to live here. I want to live with you in our own house. I want to sleep in my own bedroom."

"And you will someday," she said.

"Someday? What do you mean, someday? Are you about to run off with that jerk and just leave me here?" My emotions were swaying between anger and disbelief.

"Look, do you think this is easy for me? Everything changed after your father died. It's hard for me to find another man like him. I am the most honest, caring and loving woman in the world, but sometimes I feel like I will never find another man like your father. I'm getting old, Viviana, and it's not easy for a woman like me. Martin is the best I can do right now, and I'm not about to give him up. Not for you, not for Raven, no one. Do you understand me?"

"So, you're choosing him over me?" I asked as I smeared away an angry tear that was dripping from my left eye.

"I didn't say that. I said you have to stay here a little longer so that Martin and I can build a life for ourselves. Don't you want to see me happy again? It's not like I'm not including you. I'm just telling you that you have to wait."

"I feel like I've been waiting all of my life, Mom," I said as more tears began flowing.

"Oh, stop being such a crybaby. You're not a sappy girl. You're tough, and you need to stop acting like you're a victim. I've never once left you in a bad place. I've never left you in a shelter or homeless on the street. I've always made sure that you were staying in places much nicer than I could provide for you, and you want to try and make me feel bad because it? What the hell, Viviana?" My mother was now yelling at me.

Feeling the need to match her anger, I said, "You're my mother! You're supposed to take care of me."

"Excuse me." Aunt Raven came outside. "Why don't you two come in here and have that discussion? I don't want you to disturb my neighbors."

"What? Are you embarrassed by me, Raven?" my mother snapped at her. A few minutes ago my mom seemed reasonable, but now it was as if no matter how polite Aunt Raven was to her, she saw everything she said as a personal attack on her.

"No, but you do need to lower your voice," said Aunt Raven. My mother gave her sister a nasty look before turning her attention back to me.

"Look. It is what it is, okay? You just have to do what you've got to do until Martin and I get settled in." She wasn't about to alter her decision.

"Hey, darling, are you about set to hit the road?" asked Martin, who'd walked outside.

Aunt Raven cut her eyes at him before stepping back inside.

"Yeah. She didn't give me any money, so we'll have to think of something else," said my mom as he moved toward the vehicle. She turned to me again. "Like I said, it is what it is. I'm practically leaving you at a vacation hot spot. You have food, a roof over your head, and you're not with strangers. I'll call when I get a chance."

My mother kissed me on the forehead and walked toward Martin, who was standing next to his pickup truck, waiting for her. Once my mother was in the truck, he fired up the motor, which roared louder than the horn of a freight train. A cloud of blue smoke exited the exhaust pipe and billowed through the air. Martin backed the truck out of the driveway and into the street. Before long, he and my mother were gone. Even though I'd stopped crying and gotten my emotions in check, I felt very numb.

My mother didn't know or seem to care about how hard it was for me. It wasn't easy to be around Maya and wish that I was her. I wanted a mother and father. I wanted to live in a nice house and have friends to hang out with. I wanted to wear expensive clothes, have a cute boyfriend and not have to worry about anything. She just didn't seem to understand that although I was staying with family, it was by no means easy.

I went back inside the house and headed toward Anna's room. As I walked through the kitchen, Aunt Raven stopped me.

"Viviana, honey. Do you want to talk about it?" she asked.

I swallowed down my feelings and held my chin up. "No. I'm cool."

Seemingly satisfied with my brief answer, Aunt Raven said, "Okay."

When I entered Anna's room, she was sitting on the floor, painting her toenails green.

"What's up?" I asked.

"Nothing. Just waiting for the results of a lie detector test," Anna said.

"Lie detector test?" The words rushed out of my mouth.

"Yeah, I'm not sure which show it is, but this guy who is nineteen has been cheating on his girlfriend who is seventeen," Anna said as she focused on painting her pinkie toe. "Can you turn up the volume? The television remote is right there." Anna pointed to the floor beside her. I picked up the remote and turned up the sound when the show came back on.

"What's going on with this chick?" I asked, noticing this girl who was wearing an incredibly ugly dress and a bad wig.

"She's pregnant for a second time by her boyfriend. She already has a six-month-old son," Anna explained.

"Why would anyone want to date her? She isn't even cute," I said.

"I don't know, but her boyfriend is hot. Anyway, she says that she loves him and wants him to be a father to their children," Anna said.

"Oh, he is cute," I said when I saw the ugly girl's boyfriend come onto the stage. "Hopefully the babies will turn out looking like him," I said, laughing. Anna found my comment just as humorous. The talk show host asked the boyfriend if he'd ever beaten up his girlfriend. He answered, "Yeah. She tries to put her hands on me, and I have to defend myself." The boyfriend was making gestures with his hands.

"What a jerk," Anna said, looking up at the screen.

"Yeah, but he is a fine one," I said, checking him out more. "Do you know who he reminds me of?"

"No. Who?" Anna asked.

"Misalo. Maya's ex-boyfriend," I said.

"Oh, God, please don't say that too loudly. She's all whacked-out now that he's dumped her," Anna said.

"Well, that relationship wasn't as ideal as she claimed it was," I said, feeling absolutely no remorse for the role I'd played in ruining Maya's perfect world.

"Hand me the remote. This guy is irritating me, trying to justify beating up his baby mama," said Anna

"Don't worry. I'll switch the channel for you," I said, aiming the remote at the television.

"Hey, I wanted to tell you that the thing with you not earning enough credits at school... Don't sweat it. If you stay here and enroll in school with me, I'll help you, okay?" Anna said.

I sighed. "Thank you. It looks like I'll be here for a while. My mom just left and basically orphaned me," I reluctantly admitted.

"She was here? Why didn't you come get me? I would have loved to have talked to her," Anna complained.

"Uh, it wasn't the type of visit that was a pleasant one. She and your mom pretty much got into a nasty spat."

"Really?" Anna asked, surprised.

"Yeah, really. Anyway, I don't want to talk about that

right now," I said, pausing on the show called *That's So Raven.*

"I think it would be so cool to be clairvoyant like Raven. Then I'd be able to see into the future," Anna said.

"Yeah, I'd love to have that ability, as well," I said as Anna screwed the cap back onto her nail polish.

"Why are you painting your toes that color?" I asked. "It doesn't really work for your skin tone."

"Because I like it," Anna simply said.

"Speaking of liking things, do you still like Carlo as much as you did before?" I asked.

"I told you. I'm done with that. I don't want anything to do with him," Anna said convincingly.

"Can I ask a personal question?"

"Sure," she said.

"What was it like? I mean, being sick from the crystal meth."

"It was horrible. I just remember feeling very disoriented. The room started spinning around, and my body just did whatever it wanted to without my permission."

"That's when you had the seizure," I said.

"I wouldn't wish that feeling on my worst enemy," Anna said.

"Well, I'm just happy that you're okay," I said.

"So am I."

"So, what are you going to do with the rest of your day?" I asked.

"I was thinking about going to the Heritage Festival and hanging out. Other than that, I have no real plans," Anna said.

"Will there be any guys there?" I asked.

"Yeah, there will be plenty. People from all around come to it. There are even a lot of local bands, singers and all types of artists who perform. I think you'd like it," Anna said.

"I am so stressed-out right now. Seriously, I would enjoy going there just to help me forget about everything that's been bothering me," I said, moving across the room to glance out of Anna's window. I saw Maya and Keysha walking away from the house.

"Okay, we could go together," Anna suggested.

"Are you sure you want to go with me and not with one of your girlfriends?" I asked. After seeing Maya and Keysha together, I thought that I was becoming a nuisance and preventing Anna from hanging out with her friends.

"If we go, I plan on calling two of my girlfriends. We could meet them there, and I could introduce you to them," Anna said.

"I'd like that a lot," I said as I moved away from the window.

Four

MAYA

Keysha and I walked from my house toward Veterans Park, where the festival was being held. As we got closer, we saw throngs of people walking rhythmically into the park, many of them carrying lawn chairs and ice coolers, in search of the perfect spot to set up. There were little kids with painted butterflies on their faces and balloons tied to their wrists. I noticed several teen couples holding hands and kissing each other. That saddened me because it reminded me of how I felt when I was with Misalo. As Keysha and I made our way past a gathering of girls, we both noticed how they looked at us and started laughing for no apparent reason.

"What was that about?" Keysha asked.

"I have no idea," I said as I kept moving forward.

"I heard that there is supposed to be a fireworks show tonight," Keysha mentioned.

"I don't know if I want to be out here that late. I didn't bring any bug spray, and you know that we have mosquitoes the size of airplanes around here."

"Oh, girl, the mosquitoes aren't thinking about you.

They have way too many people to chew on," Keysha said jokingly.

I would've laughed, but I honestly just wasn't in the mood.

"Do you want to grab something from the concession stand?" Keysha asked.

"I guess," I said nonchalantly.

Keysha ordered cheese nachos and a Coke. I ordered a pretzel and a drink. Once we had our food, we located an empty picnic table and sat down to eat. As Keysha enjoyed her nachos, I casually glanced around to see who I knew. It didn't take me long to spot Priscilla. She'd just stepped away from the concession stand with a hot dog. Our eyes made contact, and she walked toward me.

"Is it okay if I sit here with you guys for a minute?" she asked.

"Hey, Priscilla," Keysha greeted her. It was cool to see that they'd let all the bad blood between them disappear. However, if Priscilla had ruined my prom dress and my evening the way she'd messed up Keysha's, I'd still be ticked off. I guess Keysha was more forgiving than I was when it came to stuff like that.

"How's the baby doing?" Keysha asked.

"Please! I don't want to talk about that right now," Priscilla said.

"Girl, isn't it about time to get your perm touched up?" Keysha asked, glancing at Priscilla's hair, which was looking like a bird's nest.

"Yes, it is, but every dime I have needs to be saved to buy things for the baby. So, right now I can't afford to see a beautician."

"Hasn't Antonio stepped up and started being a real man yet? I mean, if you had a little help, perhaps things would be different," I said.

"No. He still doesn't believe it's his. He is going to deny it until the baby arrives and he can have a blood test done. I can't believe how I fell for his bull," Priscilla said, taking a bite out of her hot dog.

"Are you craving anything yet?" Keysha asked.

"Girl, Chinese food. I swear, the owners at Ming Chow know me by name," Priscilla said with a chuckle.

"Is your stomach showing yet?" I asked.

"Thank God, no. I would hate to be all big and pregnant over the summer," Priscilla admitted.

"But that means that during the school year you'll start showing," Keysha pointed out.

"I know," Priscilla murmured. I could tell she wasn't very proud of that. "You know, when my dad found out I'd gotten pregnant, he cried." Priscilla took a deep breath, exhaled and then stopped eating. "That was the first time I'd ever seen my dad cry," she added, getting emotional.

Keysha and I looked at each other and then at her. Neither one of us knew what to do, so we didn't say a word.

"I'm sorry," Priscilla took a napkin and dabbed at the tears in her eyes. "I didn't plan on breaking down."

"It's okay," I said, giving her a hug.

"Thanks," she said, holding back more tears of regret. After getting her emotions under control, she said, "By the way, I wanted to tell you that you need to be careful about who you send photos to."

"What are you talking about?" I asked as a feeling of dread filled my heart.

"Everyone knows about the photos of you posing in your underwear. I've also overheard girls saying mean things about you."

"Mean things like what?" Keysha asked.

"Yeah, like what?" I chimed in.

"Well, this one girl got upset because her boyfriend showed her the photos and he wanted her to do the same thing for him and she got really mad at him," Priscilla said.

"I could just choke Misalo!" I hissed.

"There's more," Priscilla continued. "I want you to be careful because people can be very mean."

"I'm not worried about what people say," I said.

"But you should be. Look at me. Before I got pregnant, I used to have friends. Now those friends have told me that their parents don't want them hanging around me. They think I might be a bad influence. It sucks how some people can treat a pregnancy as if it's the plague." Priscilla started getting emotional once again.

Both Keysha and I remained silent. I didn't think we'd given much thought to how a pregnancy or even texting could ruin your reputation. Neither Keysha nor I knew what to make of Priscilla sharing so much of herself.

"Just don't let people label you as some kind of sex-crazed girl. Ever since people found out I'm pregnant, boys have been trying to have sex with me. They say stupid stuff like, 'I can't get you pregnant twice.' It's so annoying and humiliating. One jackass even took a photo of his privates with his cell phone and came up and showed it to me. I told him if he ever did it again, I'd call the cops."

"OMG. I've gotten text messages from shirtless guys trying to hook up with me," I confessed.

"For real?" Keysha asked.

"Yeah," I said.

"Who? Do you still have the pictures?" Keysha wanted to know.

"No. I deleted them. They were gross," I said.

"See, that's what happens when you get a bad reputation. Other girls are the worst. One crazy girl wanted to fight me because her boyfriend was pressuring her. I don't know how or why, but somehow she got it in her head that when I announced that I was pregnant at the prom, her boyfriend suddenly wanted her to be more like me."

"How does that happen?" Keysha asked.

Priscilla rolled her eyes. "For the life of me, I just don't understand how people get stuff twisted. I swear, sometimes I know exactly how President Obama feels. If they could blame natural disasters on him, they would."

"Wow," I said. I had never thought about what she was going through. Priscilla finished her hot dog, and the three of us sat around and chatted for about twenty minutes.

Then, all of a sudden, Priscilla said, "My stomach feels horrible."

"Are you okay?" Keysha asked.

"I just feel like I want to vomit…" A sour expression formed on Priscilla's face.

"Maybe you ate a bad hot dog," I said.

"No, it's not that. It's morning sickness," Priscilla explained. "Look, my house is just across the street. My mom is there. I'll see you guys around."

"Do you want us to walk you back?" I asked.

"No," Priscilla said, rising up. She took a hard swallow, looked both of us in the eyes and said, "I'll see you guys around." I watched as Priscilla walked toward the edge of the park.

Keysha and I finished eating our food and decided to walk around and explore everything at the festival. We looked at clothing, trinkets and other merchandise. We came across a vendor who sold all types of hats. Keysha decided that she wanted to check it out. She and I both tried on several summer hats that we thought were cute.

"Ooh, that one makes you look grown and sexy, Maya," she said as I tugged at the brim of a hat I'd tried on. Keysha picked up one just like it and tried it on.

"Now, you know that's against the rules, right?" I asked.

"I know. I don't want to walk around looking like your twin," she said jokingly. Keysha looked at herself in the mirror. "Oh, God, I look like my mother wearing this thing." She immediately took it off and put it back.

We moved along to another vendor, who was selling sunglasses. Keysha picked up a pair, tried them on, turned and looked at me for approval.

"Oh, you look like such a diva in those," I said, complimenting her.

"Really?" she asked, searching for a mirror.

"Yeah. You look like a woman who has it all together. Especially with the head scarf you have on."

Keysha found a mirror, glanced at herself and began making kissy face gestures.

"I do look kind of cute," she said, removing the sunglasses to check the price. "I think I'm going to get them. Do you see anything that you want?" she asked.

"No. I'm not really shopping for myself. I want to find something for Misalo," I said, looking around at the other vendors to see where I could go. I spotted a guy who was spray painting T-shirts. "Keysha, I'll be over there." I pointed to where I'd be.

"Okay. I'll catch up with you," she said as I stepped away.

I made my way over to the artist merchant. There were a number of people looking over his shoulder at what he was creating. When I got a chance to take a peek, I realized that he was finishing up a T-shirt with a caricature drawing of Sabrina and Keysha's brother, Mike. Mike and Sabrina were sitting on a stool. Sabrina was sitting on his lap with her cheek pressed to his face and her arm draped over his shoulder.

"You guys are going to love the way this has turned out," I said, admiring how well the designer had captured their features.

When the designer finished, Mike paid him while Sabrina and I stood off to the side.

"Hey, Maya. How are you?" Sabrina asked.

"I'm hanging," I said, trying not to sound depressed.

"I'm sorry about you and Misalo. I heard about what happened," she said.

"Thanks, but it's not over just yet." I didn't want her sympathy.

"Even after what he did to you? I mean breaking up is one thing, but doing what he did was just wack." Sabrina looked at me as if I were dumb for even wanting him back.

"I love Misalo, okay? I've been with him for a long time, and you just don't walk away when things get tough," I told her, pleading my case.

"What's up?" Mike asked as he walked up and handed Sabrina the T-shirt. While Sabrina was focused on the T-shirt, I noticed Mike glancing at me with lust in his eyes.

"Oh, God! Not you, too!" I said with disgust.

Shrugging his shoulders, Mike said, "What?"

"You were just undressing me with your eyes, Mike. You saw the photos, didn't you?" I asked.

Mike nervously glanced at Sabrina and then back at me.

"Come on. Be honest," I said, urging him to tell me the truth.

Choosing his words carefully, Mike said, "One of the guys on the football team showed them to me. I told him he should delete them." I knew Mike was lying through his teeth, but there wasn't a thing I could do about it.

"Well, I got the text photos, too. As soon as I saw the first picture, I started hitting the delete button," said Sabrina. "Me, personally, I think you're very brave for even coming out in public. You know how rumors spread around this town. People can take something as innocent as the sun shining and twist it into a story about a giant meteorite on a collision course with Earth. But I understand why you took the pictures. I know exactly what true love feels like. I took some sexy photos for Mike.

I'm just so glad he kept his promise and didn't forward them to all of his immature friends."

"Well, Misalo said the same thing. I still haven't found out why he did it," I said.

"When I saw him earlier, I was going to ask him the same thing, but the moment I mentioned your name, he cut me off. He said that he didn't want to talk about you at all," Mike informed me.

"Wait, what do you mean, when you saw him earlier?" I asked.

"He's here walking around somewhere," Mike replied, confirming what I was thinking.

"Seriously?" I asked, glancing around the crowd and searching for him.

"Hey, guys. What's up?" asked Keysha, who'd come over after paying for her sunglasses.

"Damn! Those big-ass glasses make you look like a fly." Mike insulted Keysha and then started laughing.

"That's not funny, Mike," Sabrina said, elbowing him in the ribs.

"Forget you, Mike." Keysha punched his shoulder several times.

"I was just joking. Jeez! Calm down," Mike said as he moved away from Keysha.

"Where are you guys headed?" Keysha asked Sabrina and Mike.

"We're going to the concession stand to get some food. Do you guys want to come with us?" Sabrina asked.

"No, we just came from there," Keysha informed them. "I actually just saw Wesley, and he wanted me to head

over to the main stage to watch some type of performance," she announced.

"We were over there earlier, when a local dance school
was performing. It was mostly little kids, though," Mike
said.

"Do you think Misalo is over there?" I asked.

"He might be. He was walking in that direction when
I last saw him," Mike said.

"Well, that's where Keysha and I are headed," I said.

"Cool. We'll see you guys later," said Sabrina as she
looped her arm around Mike's waist and began tugging
him along.

"Peace." Mike held up his first and second fingers as
he and Sabrina backed away.

Keysha and I made our way over to the main stage.
There were large banners with the logos of the corpo-
rate sponsors, speakers, microphones and an assortment
of musical equipment. Tan metal foldaway chairs were
neatly organized in rows, ten seats across and ten seats
deep. All the seats were nearly filled.

"Look. Two people are getting up from those front-
row seats," Keysha pointed out.

We picked up our pace to ensure that we got the prime
spot. Once we got situated, I took a glance around in
search of Misalo, but I did not see him.

"So, what's this all about, Keysha?" I asked as we
watched a musician sit down and begin slapping his palms
against bongos.

"I have no idea. In fact, I was very surprised to see that
Wesley was out of rehab," Keysha confessed.

"How did he look?" I asked.

"Really good," she answered.

"So, like, where is Lori? Why wasn't she attached to him?" I asked.

Keysha chuckled. "I asked the same question. I was, like, 'So, where is your shadow?' Wesley grimaced when I mentioned Lori. He said that she went back to Indianapolis to visit her family."

"So, he's still dating her?" I asked.

"According to him, he dumped her," Keysha said.

Before long, a man appeared onstage. He walked up to a microphone that was positioned center stage. He adjusted the height of the stand and gave the microphone a few taps with the pads of his fingers to make sure it was on.

"Thank you for coming out and spending your afternoon with us here at today's festival. My name is Omar, and I'm one of the many organizers of this event. This year I wanted to do something different. I wanted to showcase some local spoken word artists. I hope you enjoy their work and what they have to say. First up is Candice. She's a freshman at Illinois State University."

"I used to see her around Thornwood when she was a senior. I never knew she was a poet, though," said Keysha.

"Hello, everyone," Candice said, greeting the audience. She was wearing a cute blue and white top with a matching miniskirt. She looked as if she was about to say something really interesting. "This piece is called 'Standing There.'"

He's standing with her now.
And I'm remembering the way he used to be when he was with me.
Tell me. While you're standing there with her, are you thinking about me?
Do you remember slow dancing with me? Do you remember what you said to me?
You used to kiss the crevices of my tortured heart. You used to look into my eyes and tell me all the things I needed to hear but didn't care to listen to.
Do you ever think about me when you're with her?
Because I think about you. I think about you the way moonlight thinks about stars. I think about you the way hearts think about love. I think about you the way a soul thinks about finding a mate.
I'm going to tell you what I really think about her.
She's the knockoff of Chanel.
The prototype for everything I was to you.
She is a copycat.
She will never fill the void in your soul the way that I did.
Neither of you will ever know the pain I felt as I listened to you tell her
"I Do."

The audience clapped for her because it truly was a very good poem.

Keysha leaned in close to me and whispered, "She was all up on your street with that line about 'I think about you the way a soul thinks about finding a mate.'"

"Well, it's true. I can't help the way my heart feels," I stated.

Omar came back on the stage. "Okay, moving right along. Next, we have Wesley."

"OMG," Keysha said as a smile spread across her face. Wesley walked up to the microphone.

"I'm a little nervous," he said as he scanned the crowd. The moment his eyes found Keysha, he smiled. "The poem I'm about to read is called 'Keysha's Heart,' and I'd like to dedicate it to a very special friend." He nodded in Keysha's direction to let her know that he was referring to her.

Keysha got all giddy. She sat upright and listened attentively. Omar sat down at the bongos and began playing, making light background sounds for Wesley's piece.

"This is something I wrote the very first time that I saw you, but I only recently finished it," Wesley said before he began.

I am fascinated and captivated by your mystery and secrets.
I want to know who you are and what part of heaven you come from.
I want the combination to your heart so that I can make your emotions my own.
Whenever I think about you, my heart and soul soar like an eagle.
Your smile is like warm sunshine on my face.
Whenever it rains, it reminds me of all the tears I've caused you to shed.
Your teardrops burst inside my soul and remind me of how much we've been through.
My heart wants to dance with your heart and tell it how sorry I am.

My soul sings for you and my mind is consumed with thoughts of us
being together as one once again.
I once read that the first step toward healing is learning to forgive.
I hope you can forgive me so that I can walk one more step closer to you.

I glanced at Keysha and noticed her eyes brimming with moisture. I opened my purse and handed her a tissue.

"That was so beautiful." Keysha wiped away a teardrop. "Wasn't that sweet?" she asked, glancing back at me.

"Yes, it was nice," I acknowledged as the next poet came onto the stage. In the back of my mind, I was wishing Wesley was Misalo, apologizing to me. Keysha and I sat and listened to several more spoken word artists.

When that segment of the program concluded, Keysha said, "Come on. I want to go talk to Wesley about his performance."

"You go ahead. I'm going to run to the bathroom. I'll come back," I said.

"Okay." Keysha was on such an emotional high that she damn near levitated toward the rear of the stage, where the performers were.

"Oh, God," I mumbled to myself. "I hope she isn't planning on trying to hook back up with him. That would just be too crazy." I asked one of the security guards where the portable bathroom was, and she pointed me in the right direction. As I walked across the field and maneuvered my way through the crowd, I thought I saw Misalo off in a distance, talking to someone. It was difficult to confirm whether or not it was him because of my position and the size of the crowd.

"Misalo," I called, hoping he'd turn in the direction of my voice, but he couldn't hear me over the noisy crowd. I was finally able to move to a better position and confirm that it was him. He was hugging some girl.

"Who in the hell is that?" I asked myself as I rushed toward them. As I got closer and saw who he was with, I blurted out, "Oh, hell no!" and quickened my pace.

"Can I talk to you for a minute?" I asked, tugging on his arm.

"Uh, excuse you. I do believe you're being very rude," said Viviana.

"You need to stay away from him. You two don't have a thing to talk about," I snapped at her.

"Look, Maya. Why don't you go hang out with Carlo? That's who you really want," said Misalo.

I tried to get him to look into my eyes so that he could see the truth. He turned his cheek to me. He couldn't even bring himself to meet my gaze.

"Is that what you think?" I asked.

"Please. You want Carlo more than a bee wants a pot of honey," Viviana said, as if she were a credible authority on what I wanted.

I stepped in front of Misalo, raised my voice and pointed my finger in Viviana's face. "You know what? You need to stay out of my business, trick!"

"Get your finger out of my face, Maya!" Viviana snarled, issuing a threat.

"And if I don't?" I encouraged her to make a move

on me. I was all set to beat her down for even talking to Misalo.

"You know what? I'm going to be the bigger person today. Besides, it's obvious that Misalo wants nothing to do with you. He didn't even hang around to listen to your annoying voice." Viviana laughed at me condescendingly.

I looked over my shoulder, and sure enough, Misalo had walked away. I scanned the crowd but could not locate him.

"Obviously, you don't have a clue as to what it takes to keep a man," Viviana remarked as she turned and began walking away.

"Go to hell, Viviana!"

"I've already been there. It's your turn now, honey," she said, flipping up her middle finger at me.

I was literally about to rush up to her and beat her down, but I saw my little sister, Anna, approaching her and decided against it, at least for right now.

FIVE

VIVIANA

I couldn't believe how Maya had come out of a bag just because I was talking to Misalo. She really had a lot of nerve. The fact of the matter was that Misalo had approached me. Right after Anna left for the concession stand, he appeared out of nowhere and tapped me on my shoulder. When I turned to see who was trying to get my attention, I was actually nervous when I saw that it was him. I thought he'd somehow figured out I'd forwarded the photos he had of Maya in his phone.

"Viviana, right?" he asked.

"Yes," I answered, feeling apprehensive.

"I just wanted to thank you again for showing me what Maya is all about. I know it could not have been easy for you to snitch on your own cousin." Misalo had such a look of sincerity in his eyes. I almost felt guilty for causing him pain. I stood there making mental notes of his every feature. He wasn't a bad-looking guy. He had kissable lips, dreamy eyes and, from what I could tell, a really decent personality. He was a little on the skinny side, but since he was muscular, he didn't really look too scrawny. He clearly was much different than any guy I'd ever been with. He certainly wasn't the thug type, but with a little help from me, I was certain I could wrinkle up his smooth edges and turn him into my own personal bad boy.

"I don't like it when good people get hurt," I lied. I could've cared less about his feelings at the time, but now that he was single again, my position had changed.

"I still can't believe I was such a fool." A glum expression spread across his face.

"It's nothing. Everybody plays the fool sometimes. At least that's what my daddy used to tell me," I said, stepping closer to him. I placed the palm of my hand on his back, between his shoulders, and rubbed away some of his tension.

"Sounds like he was a very smart man," Misalo said. When he recognized my father as being brilliant, he instantly earned points with me.

"Yes. My daddy was the best father a girl could ever wish to have," I said proudly.

"Perhaps I'll meet him someday," Misalo said.

I was stunned by his comment. I'd never in my life met a boy who actually said he wouldn't mind meeting my dad. Misalo earned serious points with me for that. As much as I didn't want to admit it, I was starting to see why Maya was fond of him.

"I'd love for you to meet him, but he passed away," I said, releasing a sigh. Whenever I thought about my father, it always saddened me.

"Oh, I'm sorry. I didn't know," he replied, immediately apologizing.

For the life of me, I couldn't explain what possessed me

to step closer to him and hug him. Perhaps I just needed a hug at that moment. I didn't know. I was relieved when he didn't push me away and returned the gesture.

"It's okay." His words were comforting. "Maybe we'll have a chance to hang out someday. Then you could tell me what he was like."

I pulled back and gazed in Misalo's eyes to see if he was sincere. When I did, all I saw was pure honesty. I was so caught up with the fact he had any interest in me at all that I didn't see Maya racing toward us. I couldn't believe how absolutely rude she was, barging in on our conversation the way she had. I mean seriously, if Misalo still wanted to be with her, he would have been. Regardless of the video clip I'd shown him of Maya slow dancing with Carlo, the fact remained that Maya had crossed the line. I certainly didn't encourage her to hook up with Carlo. She did that all on her own.

When Maya dared me to make a move on her, I was about to unload a series of hammer fists with one hand and pull her hair with the other. Just before I was about to follow through, I stopped myself because a really wicked idea formed in my mind. In an instant, I knew exactly how I was going to make her life a living hell. It was going to take guts, but if I played my cards right, I knew I could pull it off. So, instead of kicking Maya's butt in front of Misalo, I backed off because what I had in mind for her was going to hurt far worse than any punch ever could.

After I left Maya standing alone, looking really stupid, Anna and I walked to the other side of the festival, where there were carnival games and rides. We hooked up with two of Anna's friends and hopped on a fun house ride. After that, we hit the bumper cars and then got on a water-coaster ride. Once we got off of that one, our clothes were drenched.

"OMG. Look at how soaked I am," said Anna as she combed her fingers through her wet, stringy hair.

"Our clothes will dry," I said, trying to wring some of the water out of my T-shirt.

"You know what? We should get on another roller-coaster ride. The fast velocity that the cars travel at should help us get drier a lot quicker," suggested Anna.

"You're so smart," I said, complimenting her.

"It just makes sense, don't you think?" she asked.

"It does to me," I said.

We stood in line a total of four times for the roller-coaster ride. Just as Anna predicted, our clothes got dry pretty quickly.

As nightfall began to arrive, Anna and I decided to stay for the fireworks show. We found a grassy area in the middle of the baseball field with just enough space for the two of us to sit. I decided to lean back on my elbows and gaze up at the stars. I closed my eyes for a moment but quickly opened them up when I heard someone say, "Excuse me. I'm trying to get through."

I didn't move fast enough, and somehow Misalo stepped in the wrong direction and smashed my fingers.

"Ouch!" I yelled out.

"Oh, I'm so sorry. I didn't mean to step on you. It's just so crowded out here. I guess I didn't see your hand," he said, apologizing immediately. I wiggled all my fingers to make sure they still functioned.

"You'll live," Anna said as she took a peek at my fingers.

"Do you guys mind if I sit and watch the fireworks display with you?" Misalo asked.

"I don't care what you do," Anna answered him.

Misalo then looked at me.

"Yeah, I guess," I said, still wiggling the pain out of my fingers.

Misalo sat beside me and said, "Let me take a look."

He took my hand into his own and began brushing away the dirt. He seemed genuinely concerned. I focused on him instead of my fingers. The strangest thing happened the moment he touched me. The pain evaporated. I couldn't believe how caught up in his touch I got.

"You know Maya is lurking around, don't you, Misalo?" Anna asked.

I took my hand back and glanced over at Anna. It was the first time that I wished she weren't with me.

"Yeah, I saw her earlier, but I don't want to deal with her," he said.

"And you shouldn't have to, especially after the way she played you with Carlo," I said, feeling an immediate need to fuel his anger.

"I don't think I'll ever understand why you and Carlo are so hooked on Maya," Anna said, lowering her head between her shoulders and shaking it disapprovingly.

"You also knew about Carlo?" Misalo asked.

"It was so obvious," Anna said just as the night sky lit up with the first round of fireworks.

I sat there with Misalo, feeling like we were on a date. Although he didn't say much more or try anything, for some strange reason I began developing feelings for him.

I glanced at him one more time, just to be sure. The first thought that came to my mind was that we'd make a great-looking couple.

SIX

MAYA

After the fireworks show ended, Keysha, Wesley and I gathered our belongings and began heading home. Keysha had invited Wesley to hang out with us. I was disappointed that she'd invited him to our girl outing, especially since I was dying to talk to her about how I saw Viviana looking at my man like she was about to put her hooks in him. Then the way Misalo played me... I couldn't believe that he just walked away from me. What the hell was that about? In a million years I never would've thought that Misalo would treat me this way.

"You're awfully quiet. Is everything okay?" asked Wesley.

I tried not to cut my eyes at him, but I couldn't help it. "I'm fine," I answered as we walked across a parking lot filled with cars.

"She and Misalo broke up," Keysha said, filling in the blanks for him.

"Oh, no. I'm so sorry. I didn't know," Wesley replied.

"You were in rehab. You had no way of knowing," I said. I wanted my words to sting him. Although he didn't

personally do anything to me or deserve it, I felt the need
to lash out at the closest male.

"How did it happen?" asked Wesley.

"Does it really matter? And for the record, Keysha, we
haven't broken up. We just have a big misunderstanding
that needs to be worked out. I know my man. He's just in
a funny place right now and needs me more than he re-
alizes," I said, knowing my words were the honest truth.

"If you guys don't mind, I'd like to walk both of you
home," Wesley said, changing the subject.

I was about to say, "Yes, I do mind," but I knew that
would be totally rude.

"I'm cool with that," said Keysha.

I shrugged my shoulders in agreement. At that point,
I just wanted to get home.

Fifteen minutes later, I was standing at my door, saying good-night to Wesley and Keysha.

"Call me when you get in the house. I need to talk to
you," I whispered to Keysha as she gave me a hug.

"Okay," she whispered back.

"See you later, Wesley," I said before stepping inside.

I locked the door and went up to my room. I changed
clothes and freshened up, putting on my pajama outfit. I
called Misalo but got no answer. I sent him a text message
that read, If you truly ever loved me, please give me a
call. I sat on the edge of my bed with my phone, waiting
for his response. When he didn't answer right away, I felt
like crying. A short time later, my phone rang.

"Hello, Misalo?" I assumed it was him.

"No, it's me, Keysha. I made it home safely," she informed me.

"Oh," I said, releasing a disappointed sigh.

"Why did you say it like that? Didn't you have a good time?" Keysha finally picked up on the fact that I was feeling dismal.

"I saw Misalo at the festival," I said, walking over to my bedroom door and closing it.

"For real? Why didn't you tell me?" she asked.

"Duh. You were too busy entertaining Wesley," I remarked sarcastically.

"I was not all that into Wesley. I was just happy to see that he was doing well," Keysha retorted, defending her behavior.

"Could've fooled me," I remarked.

"Okay, out with it. What happened with Misalo?" Keysha asked.

"My slut of a cousin, Viviana, was trying to get way too friendly with him," I said.

"Get out of here! No way!" Keysha spoke so loudly I had to pull my phone away from my ear.

"Yeah, she was. I put a stop to that real quick. I snapped on her. I don't know who she thinks she is, but she has absolutely no need or reason to talk to Misalo," I said, fanning the flames of my anger.

"So, what did Misalo say and do?" Keysha asked.

"That's the part I'm really ticked off about. He didn't stick around. While I was busy threatening to beat Viviana down, he walked away from me," I explained.

"Wow! That doesn't seem like something Misalo would do." By the sound of her voice, I could tell that Keysha was just as perplexed as I was.

"I know. He's being a real jerk right now, but I'm hoping he at least has a good reason for the way he's treat-ing me. I have to figure out what's going on with him so that we can get through this together as a couple," I said, looking at a photo of him that I had in a scrapbook.

"Nothing that Misalo is doing makes sense. I mean, honestly, you should be ticked off with him for sending those photos of you to everyone," Keysha reminded me.

"I am mad. I'm also really hurt by what he's done, but I'm at least willing to listen to his side of the story as to why he did it. If I could understand his logic, then I'm sure I'd be able to forgive him." I paused and sighed. "Keysha, I just want things to go back to the way they were."

"How is that going to happen? Especially if he can't stand being near you."

"I don't know how, but I'll figure out something," I said.

"Maybe I'll confront him when I see him again at the pool, and ask him for a straight answer," Keysha said.

"I have an idea," I said, snapping my fingers.

"What?" Keysha asked.

"Why don't I hang around the pool with you? That way you won't have to ask him for me. I could do it my-self."

"Sounds like a plan to me," Keysha agreed.

"But wait. I have to make him really want to be near me since he seems to have forgotten how much he loves me," I said.

"I can hear your mind clicking through this phone. What's going on inside that head of yours?" Keysha asked.

"Ha. You know me too well," I said, chuckling.

"Best friends are supposed to know each other like that," Keysha said.

"Yeah, yeah, yeah," I agreed. "Okay, I want to go to the mall and find me a really hot bathing suit. Something that will make his head turn when he sees me in it."

"So, you're going to go and buy a bikini?" Keysha asked.

"Yeah. I'm thinking about a nice bikini," I said, envisioning the color and style I wanted.

"OMG. I was just thinking the same thing, because when I was at the mall, I saw one that I really wanted, but I didn't get it."

"Well, I think we need to make plans to head over to River Oaks tomorrow. What time do you work?" I asked.

"I'm on the afternoon shift, so I don't have to be at work until two o'clock."

"Cool. That gives us plenty of time. I could be at your place by ten o'clock. Is that cool?"

"Sounds like a plan to me," Keysha said, agreeing.

"Okay. I'll see you then," I said and ended our conversation.

The following day Keysha and I arrived at River Oaks Center, excited about getting some shopping done. We walked through the Sears entrance and made our way through the store and out into the mall.

"I can't wait to get my new bikini. When Misalo sees me in it, his jaw is going to hit the floor," I boasted.

"You know what would make it even sexier?" Keysha asked.

"No. What?"

"If you were to get a matching sarong to wrap around your waist. I just know you'd look dangerously hot."

"I like that idea," I said, hoping I would find something that would match.

We continued our walk through the mall until Keysha said, "Wait. I want to stop in here and look at some new sneakers. The ones I have look horrible."

We stopped at Lady Foot Locker, and we both began browsing.

"What do you think about these?" Keysha asked, holding up a purple-and-white suede shoe.

"I like the color, but I'm not too sure about the style," I said as a pink-and-gray shoe caught my eye. I picked the shoe up and was so busy inspecting it that I was startled when a sales associate asked me if I needed help.

"I'm sorry. I didn't mean to scare you, Maya."

I immediately turned to see who the sales associate was and figure out how he knew my name.

"Carlo?" I was totally shocked to see him.

"Why did you say my name like that?" he asked, smiling at me.

I toned down my voice so that I sounded more cordial. "I didn't mean anything by it. It's just that this is the last place I ever expected to see you."

"I work here. I started not too long ago," he said, glancing down at the shoe I was holding. "Would you like for me to get that in your size?"

"Uh." I couldn't believe that I'd lost my train of thought. Whenever I was around him, my brain seemed to malfunction.

Keysha came to my rescue. "What's up, Carlo?"

Snapping his fingers, he said, "Keysha, the lifeguard, right?"

"Yes. Glad to see that you have a good memory. Come on, Maya. We should go. I don't want any shoes out of here. I've changed my mind." Keysha was about to turn and walk out.

"Wait a minute," Carlo said, stopping her. "Are you sure you couldn't find anything? You haven't even been in here that long."

"I'm sure," Keysha whispered sarcastically.

"Well, okay." Carlo turned back toward me. He reached out and took my hand in his own. "I heard about how sick your sister got. I hope she's okay."

"She got poisoned at your house," Keysha quickly pointed out.

"Hey, I personally had nothing to do with my cousins bringing that over. I don't get down like that. I'm no angel, by any means, and I do have a rocky past, but I've never been down with the drug thing," Carlo said defensively.

"You could've fooled me," Keysha fired back, not willing to give Carlo any slack.

Turning back toward Keysha, Carlo said, "I truly am very sorry about what happened. If I could've prevented it, I would have. Look, to make a long story short, my family member who brought the stuff into the house has been asked not to come around anymore. What he did was very disrespectful."

"Not to mention illegal. I'm glad your family worked all of that drama out," Keysha said and signaled for me to follow her out the door.

"Let me make it up to you guys. I'd like there to be no hard feelings between us. If you buy something, I'll give you my employee discount."

"How much of a discount is it?" Keysha asked.

"Fifteen percent," Carlo said and smiled at Keysha.

"Maybe next time," Keysha said and once again motioned for me to leave with her.

I don't know what I was thinking or why I opened my mouth, but I said, "Can I see this shoe in a size seven?"

Carlo took the shoe and said, "Sure. I'll be right back."

Keysha walked over to me and whispered, "What are you doing?"

"I like that shoe. Plus, I'll get a discount. There is nothing wrong with using him for his discount," I said, justifying my selfish need.

"Are you sure you're not trying to set him up to be your rebound guy?" Keysha asked, seeking a reasonable explanation from me.

"I only want the discount for the shoes, that's all," I assured her.

"Fine," Keysha said as we both sat down.

Carlo returned with my size. He kneeled down on one knee and removed the sandals I was wearing. He then removed the shoes from the box, took out the stuffing, got socks for me and laced up the shoes. Just before Carlo slipped one of the shoes onto my foot, he said, "You have very soft feet, and I love your toenail polish." Carlo massaged the heel of my foot a little. His fingers had magic or something in them, because his touch made me feel very strange. He was about to do the same thing for the other foot, but Keysha interrupted.

"Okay, you don't have to go the extra mile here. She's a big girl and can put on her own shoes."

I glanced down at Carlo, who was still kneeling before me. He was looking at me with his gorgeous eyes. His eyes had the strangest effect on me. I couldn't even explain what I was thinking to myself, let alone anyone else.

"Will you hurry up and try on the other shoe?" Keysha's voice snapped me out of my trance.

"Yeah," I answered as I slipped my other foot into the shoe.

"How do they feel?" Carlo asked.

I stood up, walked around and looked at my feet in a nearby mirror.

"That's a nice color, don't you think, Keysha?" Carlo positioned himself next to Keysha and folded his arms.

"They're okay," I heard her say.

"I think I'm going to get them," I said, taking a seat to remove the shoes and place them back in the box.

"Okay. I'll ring the sale up," Carlo said.

"With the discount, right?" Keysha asked, making sure he held true to his word.

Carlo laughed. "Of course, Keysha. I'm serious about the discount for you, too. Are you sure you don't want to get something?"

"I'm positive," she said.

Carlo rang up my purchase, and I paid for it. As we walked out the door, Carlo said, "I hope to see you again soon, Maya."

I glanced back at Carlo, who was smiling at me.

"Girl, if you don't come on and leave him alone, I swear I'll choke you," Keysha grumbled, threatening me.

"There is no need to choke me," I said, feeling good about my purchase.

"What is it with you and him? What really went on the night you were at that party?" Keysha asked.

"Nothing, and please stop asking me that question," I told her.

"I believe you," Keysha said, "but Carlo seems like the type of guy that would have you very confused."

"I'm not interested in Carlo," I said conclusively.

"Just remember you can't have your cake and eat it, too," Keysha reminded me.

"I know," I stated as I refocused my thoughts on getting a smoking-hot bikini for Misalo.

After visiting several stores, Keysha and I found the perfect bathing suit for me. It was a blue-and-white-checked, triangle-cut Burberry-patterned bikini. Once I paid for it, we decided to stop and grab a bite to eat at the food court. I ordered a salad, and Keysha ordered a slice of pizza. We found a vacant table and sat down. No sooner had we gotten comfortable than Carlo came up, pulled over an empty chair from a nearby table and sat next to me.

"What's up, ladies? It looks like we meet again," said Carlo, smiling.

"Does the term 'a fly at a picnic' mean anything to you?" Keysha had clearly become annoyed with Carlo.

"No, it doesn't." Carlo chuckled.

"What are you doing here?" I asked.

"I'm on my lunch break," he said.

"Well, why don't you go buy some food and eat somewhere else?" Keysha was clearly being rude.

"Oh, it's like that? I'm good enough to use for my employee discount, but not nice enough to sit at a lunch table with you." Carlo was, without question, offended.

"No, it's not like that," I said, wanting to avoid a conflict.

"Good, because I'd hate to think that you guys were just a couple of users." Carlo was right. It wouldn't be very nice of me to use him the way I had and then turn my back on him.

"Why don't you go get something to eat and join us?" I suggested. I glanced at Keysha, who looked baffled by what I'd just said.

"I'll get something in a minute," Carlo said as he looked at my shopping bag. "What else did you buy today?" Without asking for permission, Carlo reached into my shopping bag and pulled out my swimsuit. "Wow! That's going to look so hot on you," he said, pressing the bra top against me.

"Would you please put her things back in her bag!" Keysha said, clenching her teeth.

"I'm just trying to give her a compliment," Carlo said, then placed the item back in the bag and rested his hand on the back of my chair. "You should let me taste some of your salad." He leaned in closer to me.

I looked at him, then at Keysha. The look I saw in her eyes was one of panic. I tried to figure out why she was darting her eyes back and forth, but the signals she was sending didn't make sense to me, until I felt someone tap me on my shoulder. I looked up and saw Misalo.

"Can I talk to you for a minute?" Misalo said.

"Yo, man, don't you think you're being a little disrespectful? Don't you see me talking to her?" Carlo's voice had an edge to it as he fired blades with his eyes at Misalo.

"This has nothing to do with you. This is a conversation between me and Maya. So get lost." I'd never heard Misalo sound so forceful before.

Carlo rose to his feet and sized Misalo up.

"Oh, boy," Keysha said nervously as she rose to her feet and gathered up her things.

"Maya," Misalo called. I looked at him and was about to step away with him.

"Maya," Carlo called. I glanced over my shoulder at him. He puckered his lips and blew me a kiss. "I can't wait to see you again. If you need me to do anything else for you, and I do mean anything, just let me know."

Misalo completely lost it when Carlo said that. He stepped around me and positioned himself in front of Carlo.

"What are you going to do?" Carlo fearlessly taunted Misalo.

"All I know is…" Misalo was so angry, he didn't finish his thought. Instead he shoved Carlo. Carlo responded by shoving him back. Misalo lunged for Carlo, and they both crashed into a table, knocking it over. They tumbled to the floor, each of them slinging wild punches and tugging on each other's clothes.

"Oh, my God!" I yelled out as Misalo and Carlo rolled around on the floor, trying to establish control over one another.

"Damn!" I heard Keysha say as she moved toward me.

Several mall security guards came rushing over. Within

moments, at least five mall cops had arrived to break up the disturbance.

"You're not so bad," Misalo snarled at Carlo.

"This isn't over, idiot!" Carlo answered back as he was being restrained.

As Misalo was being held, he spit on the floor. I glanced down at his saliva and saw that there was blood in it.

"Misalo, are you hurt?" I asked. I tried to approach him, but a mall cop stopped me. Misalo was escorted away before he could answer. I turned my attention back to Carlo and noticed that he was being taken in a different direction.

seven

VIVIANA

I was in the backyard, resting on a hammock. The warm air felt great on my skin, and the scent of freshly cut grass and flowers in full bloom hung in the air. It was a perfect day for doing absolutely nothing. I looked at the blue sky and the white clouds gently floating along. One cluster of clouds took the form of a unicorn. Another cluster looked like a car. It was funny how clouds could do that. I listened as a red cardinal sang its heart out. I scanned the nearby tree branches for the red-and-black bird. When I found the little guy, I laughed to myself, because the cardinal appeared to have a Mohawk as a hairstyle. I was fascinated by how something so small could make so much noise.

I turned my attention back to the white, fluffy clouds, which had once again changed their shape. This time I was sort of freaked out by what I saw. I swear, the clouds had formed into the face of my father. I blinked my eyes a few times to make sure they weren't playing tricks on me, but no matter how much I tried to refocus, the clouds still appeared to have the face of my dad. I missed him so much. When I was a little girl, I loved being with him.

The moment I heard him pick up his keys, I'd rush to his side.

"I want to go," I'd say.

In my mind I could hear his voice say, "Vivi, I'm only walking to the corner store."

"Please, Papa," I'd beg him as I sat on the floor with my back against the wall and put on my fancy white shoes.

He'd smile at me and say, "No, not those shoes. Put on your gym shoes, the ones that light up."

I'd put on the other shoes, place my hand in his and walk out the door with him. I'd skip alongside of him and wave hello to everyone I saw. Some people viewed my father as a badass because of his tattoos, white T-shirt, red bandanna and dark sunglasses. To me, he was a protector who never let harm come to me. He was my personal bodyguard in a neighborhood that was very rough. He was also very sweet. Most people didn't know I was the only person who could get him to act silly. He'd let me practice braiding his hair, and if I ever played a prank on him, like hiding his door keys or taking money out of his pants pocket, he wouldn't get mad.

Sometimes, when my dad and I would go out, he'd take me to the neighborhood playground. Most times, there were guys sitting on the equipment, drinking and smoking, so kids couldn't play. However, if my father came and told them to move, they'd be very respectful and even apologize to him.

I looked back up at the clouds that resembled my father, but they were now gone. I smeared away a tear and told myself to stop being so sentimental.

As I continued to enjoy my lazy day, I decided that

I should at least give getting along with Maya one last shot. Even though I liked her about as much as I enjoyed smelling a dead skunk, I figured if we were going to be living under the same roof, we should at least be civil. I figured that once she returned from the mall, I'd be nice and ask if we could talk so that we could establish some ground rules. This way, we'd limit any misunderstandings or potential conflicts that might come up, since I clearly wouldn't be leaving anytime soon.

By early afternoon, Maya finally came strolling up the driveway with shopping bags. She had on some dark diva sunglasses and was talking on the phone through an earpiece. By that time, I was lounging around on a lawn chair, drinking Kool-Aid and surfing the internet with Aunt Raven's laptop.

"Maya, can I talk to you for a second?" I asked as she was walking by.

"Hang on a minute, Keysha." Maya glanced at me, curled her lips into a sour expression and asked, "What?"

"I want to talk to you," I told her.

"We don't have anything to talk about," Maya said with nothing but attitude. "Oh, wait. Yes, we do. You need to stay away from Misalo."

"Is that a warning?" I asked, thinking she was trying to intimidate me.

"I don't give out warnings. I only hand out promises."

"I can't help it if he likes me more than he likes you," I said defiantly. I knew that comment would rattle her cage.

"Keysha, let me call you back," she said, ending her conversation. "Misalo would never go for a hood rat like you." Maya removed her sunglasses.

"Who are you calling a hood rat?" I asked, setting the laptop aside and rising to my feet. If she kept talking to me this way, it wouldn't take long for my hair-trigger temper to kick in.

Maya looked around, as if she were searching for something or someone. "Only you and I are out here, and I know for damn sure I'm not a hood rat."

Insulted, I pointed my finger at her and said, "I've just declared war on you."

"Please. You couldn't spell the word *war* if I spotted you the letters *w* and *r.*"

"You're impossible to get along with, Maya. I was going to give you another chance, but forget it now."

"You bore me, Viviana. All you need to do is stay out of my way and stay away from Misalo. You got that?" Maya asked.

With fire in my eyes I said, "I hear you, but—"

Cutting me off, Maya said, "No more needs to be said. We're done here." She put her glasses back on and continued on her prissy little way. As she entered the house, I finished what I was going to say.

"Payback is a real beyotch, Maya, and all is fair in love and war."

By late afternoon, I'd created Twitter and MySpace accounts. I'd just finished uploading photos that I'd taken with the built-in camera on the laptop to my new Facebook page. I found Anna and made her my first friend. Once she accepted, I saw that she was friends with Maya, Keysha and even Misalo. I clicked Misalo's photo and then forwarded a friend request to him. I was completely surprised when, less than twenty seconds later, a message popped up, informing me he'd accepted my request.

"Damn, that was quick," I mumbled to myself. I looked at his profile page and then clicked on his photos. There were a ton of photos of him and Maya at various events. I clicked the video link to see what he'd posted. There were a bunch of videos of him playing soccer. There was another one of him and Maya walking along a wooded trail. Misalo was videotaping Maya as she walked in front of him. The video must've been taken last fall, because there were brown leaves everywhere and the trees were bare. Maya was wearing shorts and a short-sleeved pink top, so it must've been one of the last warm days before it became bone-chillingly cold.

On the video, Misalo jokingly said, "We're all alone in the woods. A killer could come and murder us."

"I'd let him kill you first," Maya said.

"You'd let me get killed?" Misalo asked sadly.

"Wouldn't you want me to live?" Maya countered as she kicked at a cluster of brown leaves that were at her feet.

"Of course I would. I put you before everything," Misalo acknowledged. "But would you at least go for help?"

"Of course I would." Maya turned and looked directly into the camera and blew him a kiss.

"Gross!" I said aloud. *How can he stand for her to kiss him?* I wondered.

The two of them came to a creek. Maya decided to walk to the creek's edge. She asked, "Isn't this beautiful scenery?"

"Not as beautiful as you," Misalo answered. When he said that, I almost gagged.

"You're so sweet," Maya said as she walked back toward him from the creek's edge. "Let me videotape you." She took hold of the camera. Misalo stepped into the video frame. He looked cute. His blue jeans were sagging, and he had on a long red shirt with a gold chain draped around his neck. His hair was freshly cut, and when he smiled at the camera, I felt as if he were smiling at me instead of Maya.

"Do you know what we should do out here?" Misalo asked.

"If you say 'Have sex,' or anything like that, I swear I'm going to hit you on the head with this camera," Maya warned him.

"What a prude," I mumbled. "You could at least make out a little. What's wrong with that?"

"Okay, there went that thought." Although Misalo said it jokingly, I knew he had to have felt the burn of rejection. "We could have fun in a different way," he suggested.

"How?" Maya asked.

"We could do our own version of *The Blair Witch Project*." He laughed.

"You want me to run through the woods, screaming, trip and film the snot running out of my nose? I don't think so," Maya proclaimed, as if it were the dumbest idea she'd ever heard.

I whispered to myself, "I'd be cool with at least pretending something was after me. What harm would that do? Jeez! She's more of a stick-in-the-mud than I thought."

The video ended and I clicked on the next one. It was a prom video. I could hear Keysha's voice in the background, directing them to stand close together.

"You guys look so hot," I heard Keysha say over the loud roar of the music and the crowd.

Misalo looped his arm around Maya and smiled.

"Okay, you need to kiss her or something, Misalo," Keysha directed him.

He started laughing. Once he stopped, he turned toward Maya, pulled her close to him and kissed her.

Keysha filmed it for all of two seconds before turning the camera toward herself. She then said, "That's true love." When she turned the camera back toward Misalo and Maya, they were slow dancing.

I clicked on the next video clip and saw Maya standing alone.

"Okay, I think I can still do this," she said, just before spinning around on one foot like a ballerina. I was hoping she'd fall flat on her face, but she didn't. She smiled at the camera. Princess Maya looked too damn happy, and honestly, her cheerfulness made my stomach turn.

I was about to click on the next video when the chat screen popped up. It was Misalo. His message to me said, I didn't know you were on Facebook.

I answered, I just joined today. You're my second friend.

I see. Nice profile picture, he replied.

I answered, Thank you. I don't look too weird, do I?

No, not at all. I'm sure plenty of guys will friend you and send you messages, he wrote.

Is that a compliment? I asked.

He answered, It can be.

Then that's what I will take it as, I replied. So, why aren't you with Maya?

Because she's a liar! He typed out the words in capital letters.

I was, like, "Wow!" when I saw that. I responded with a question. Do you want to talk about it? There was a long pause before he answered. For a moment, I thought I'd asked the wrong question or that he'd logged off. Finally he answered.

I still can't believe how dumb I've been. I drove to the mall today to pick up a birthday present for my mother. As I was walking past the food court, I saw Maya, Carlo and Keysha sitting together, having lunch. So, I went up to Maya and asked if I could speak to her for a moment. Then Carlo opened his mouth as if I was stepping to his girl.

Really? I asked with my fingers glued to the keyboard. I wanted to know every detail of what happened next.

Yeah, he answered.

Well, what happened? I was on edge, waiting for additional details.

It's like you said. They've been dealing with each other behind my back. I even saw him holding up a new bikini, which I assumed he bought for her. At that moment, I saw my opportunity to score points.

So I wrote, He probably did.

Yeah, I know. Anyway, Carlo threatened me, which I found to be very disrespectful. I had to defend my honor, so we got into a fight.

What! I couldn't type the word fast enough.

Mall security guards escorted us out through different exits. Next time I see him, I'm going to kick his ass. Misalo was clearly angry.

I saw yet another chance to score even bigger points and really screw up Maya's life, so I wrote, You know, I probably shouldn't tell you this. I paused and waited to see if he'd take the bait.

Tell me what? he asked.

No, I really shouldn't, I replied to string him along more.

Is it about Maya? he asked.

Yes, I answered.

Then tell me, please. I want to know.

I smiled because I was about to really twist things around. Well, I was walking back from Mr. Submarine earlier. I saw Maya and Carlo parked a few blocks from the house. They were doing some serious kissing. She was totally all over him.

No way! Misalo wrote back, not wanting to believe me.

I knew I had to make the lie stick, so I replied, I saw it with my own eyes. Why would I lie? Come on, Misalo, don't be so naive. You said that you saw them hugged up, having lunch together. How many more signals do you need before you realize she's treating you like a chump?

You're right, Viviana, but my heart is just having trouble believing what my eyes are telling it. I just don't know what to do or think right now.

I thought to myself, *I'm going to have to really work on him.*

Well, if I were you, the first thing I'd do is change my Facebook status to single. Then I'd delete all the photos and videos of her off of my page.

I just don't understand what I did wrong. Why is she doing this to me? he asked. I knew right then that he still had feelings for her in spite of what I'd just told him. So, I took a different approach.

Would you like for me to spy on her for you? I asked. There was another long pause before he typed anything.

Yes, he finally agreed.

In-box me your cell number, and I'll text you every time I hear or see something.

Why are you doing this for me? he asked.

Because I think you deserve a better girlfriend. One who is real and doesn't play silly games. Like, if I were your girlfriend, you'd never have to worry about me even looking at another guy. I threw that out there just to see how he'd respond.

As crazy as it sounds, I really do believe you, he wrote.

And I wouldn't be such a prude like Maya. I'd shower

you with all kinds of affection. You'd never hear me say no to you, I replied, pouring it on.

How do I know you won't play me like Maya is? She is your cousin, right? he asked.

Yeah, she's my cousin, but that doesn't mean we're exactly alike. Maya and I are totally different from each other. I would never hurt you the way Maya has.

Maya is going to reap what she sows. Now that I think about it, she has always mistreated me.

Yeah. She and Keysha have probably been laughing at you behind your back all this time.

I think you're right again because Keysha has gone through a lot of guys. At least three that I know of, Misalo wrote, finding another point to agree on.

You know, that old saying is true. Birds of a feather do flock together, I responded, proud at the way I was slinging mud.

Thank you for being so real, he wrote.

No problem, baby. I'm here for you anytime you need me, I declared.

You called me baby. Is that a good thing? he asked.

I don't know. You tell me, I wrote, placing the ball back in his court.

I think it could be a very good thing, he admitted. It was at that point I realized it would be only a matter of time before I had him eating out of the palm of my hand.

I think you're right, I replied.

Can I get your phone number, as well? he asked.

I'll send it to your email address, I wrote.

Cool. It's been nice talking to you, he replied.

Same here. I chuckled.

Keep me posted on what Maya does, okay? he asked.

Don't worry. I got you, I reassured him.

I'll holla back at you later, he wrote, ending our conversation.

I leaned back in my seat and smiled, not knowing whether to praise Jesus or thank the devil for allowing Misalo to listen to me. Either way, the war had begun, and Maya had no clue as to what was coming her way.

Eight

MAYA

The next morning, I awoke to the roar of a motorcycle passing my house. I remained in bed, resting on my stomach and thinking about Misalo. After I'd come home from the mall yesterday, I called him several times, but he didn't answer. I'd logged on to Facebook and forwarded a message to him there, as well, but got no answer. I was happy to see that the photos and videos of us were still up. However, I was disappointed by the number of in-box messages I'd gotten from boys who went to my school and who mentioned that they'd seen my photos and wanted to hook up with me. I'd then got mad with Misalo all over again for what he'd done. I'd decided that enough was enough and that I'd go to his house so we could work out our issues.

I finally sat up and walked over to my clock radio, which was on top of my dresser. I turned it on, and Tyrese was singing his latest song about lovers who were going through a difficult time.

"Sing, Tyrese," I whispered aloud as I listened to the lyrics of his song, which seemed to speak directly to me.

After the song ended, I walked toward the bathroom to freshen up. The door was closed, so I knocked.

"I'm in here," I heard Viviana shout out. I rolled my eyes and walked downstairs to use the bathroom on the lower level. I freshened up and then headed back upstairs to my bedroom to get dressed. Once I was done, I headed back downstairs and ran into my father.

"Hi, Dad," I said.

"Good morning," he greeted me. Dad looked as if he hadn't gotten much sleep.

"Are you okay?" I asked.

"Uncle Herman's allergies are bothering him," Viviana said, approaching him with a box of allergy medicine. "I'm sorry, Uncle Herman, but I think you're out of medicine."

"I'll have to make a run to the pharmacy," he said, sneezing and breathing through his mouth.

"I'll go with you," Viviana quickly offered. "I can run back upstairs and change out of my pajamas really fast."

"Oh, hell no," I muttered. *First, she tries to take Misalo, and now she's going to try to get close to my dad. I don't think so.*

"I'll go with you, Dad. I'm already dressed," I said, moving toward him and taking his hand in my own. I started moving him away from Viviana. I had to let her know that my daddy was totally off-limits to her.

"Viviana, do you want us to wait for you?" asked my father.

I turned to face Viviana. I was sure she saw the fire in my eyes.

"No. You guys go," she said as she walked toward the family room.

Now, in all honesty, I really didn't want to go to the drugstore with my father. He certainly was capable of doing that all on his own. In my heart, I wanted to tell him to just go, but if I did that, his feelings would be hurt or he might get suspicious. So, I had to delay my confrontation with Misalo.

My father and I drove to the local drugstore. He walked over to the personal care section to pick up razor blades, while I went and found his allergy medicine.

As I was searching the shelf, someone came up behind me and said, "Hey, beautiful. We've got to stop meeting like this."

Startled, I screamed.

"Calm down," Carlo said.

"Boy, I swear, you've got to stop surprising me like that," I griped.

"My bad. How are you?" he asked.

"I should be asking you that. I'm so sorry that Misalo attacked you. I didn't expect him to do that," I said.

"Because of what he did, I lost my job," Carlo explained.

"Are you serious?" I asked, suddenly feeling horrible.

"Yeah. The store manager got wind of the fight. When the mall cops kicked me out, I phoned the store to let the manager hear my side of the story. The manager brought all my belongings to the rear entrance of the store, handed them to me and fired me on the spot for what he called a mall brawl."

"That's horrible. Did you explain to him that it was self-defense?" I asked.

Shrugging his shoulders he said, "I tried, but it was no use. I really needed that job, too."

I felt so bad that I wanted to cry. I reached out and rubbed his arm, which was very muscular. "I'm so sorry," I said, apologizing again. "I wish there were something I could do. Would it help if I contacted the store manager and explained what happened?"

"I doubt it," Carlo said, swinging his head back and forth. "Do you really want to know what would make me feel better?" he asked.

"What?"

Reaching forward and taking my hand in his own, he said, "Have lunch with me."

"I'm not sure if that's such a good idea," I said, looking around to make sure my father didn't see us.

"What? Is Misalo in here, too?" Carlo asked, searching around for him.

"No," I quickly said, "but my dad is."

"Oh," Carlo responded, releasing my hand. "So, even after everything that went down, I'm not worthy of having a decent lunch with you?" I could hear the disappointment in his voice.

"Carlo, it's not that. It's just…" I looked into his eyes and found it difficult to say no to him. I sighed and said, "It's just lunch and nothing more, right?"

"That's all. I just want to have lunch and talk. Is that cool?" he asked.

"I guess, but we have to go someplace where no one will see us."

"I'm cool with that. Do you want me to come pick you up?" he asked.

"No," I quickly answered. "My father wouldn't like that very much, especially since my little sister was poisoned at your house, and you're older than me."

"Wow. I'm never going to live that one down, am I?" he asked.

"Sorry. I don't mean to keep throwing that in your face. I tell you what. Why don't I meet you at Pizza Hut later on?" I suggested.

"How much later?" he asked.

"In about an hour. How does that sound?" I asked.

"Can I get your phone number?" he asked.

"Sure," I said and gave it to him.

"Cool. I'll see you later on," he said and walked away.

I closed my eyes and exhaled. I convinced myself that it would be a harmless lunch date and that, once I did it, I wouldn't feel guilty about Carlo losing his job over me. I told myself that I would be with him for only an hour, an hour and a half at the most. Then I'd go hunt down Misalo.

When I got back home, Viviana, Anna and my brother, Paul, were sitting at the table, eating ice cream. I also noticed my mother was standing at the island counter, putting a scoop of black walnut ice cream in a bowl.

"Make me a bowl, too, baby," said my dad, who'd walked in behind me.

"Isn't that going off of your diet?" I asked playfully as I stood next to my mom.

"I'm allowed to cheat every now and again," my mom said, defending her decision to eat something fattening. I watched as she popped the top on a can of Coca-Cola and poured it over her ice cream. I watched as it fizzed in the bowl.

"Eww," I said.

"Hey, don't knock it until you've tried it," she said, bringing down another bowl for my dad. She then asked me, "Do you want some ice cream?"

"No," I said before excusing myself. I glanced over at Viviana, who seemed to be watching my every move. I wanted to ask her why the hell she was glaring at me so hard, but I didn't. I walked upstairs and into my bedroom. I shut the door and called Keysha.

"What's up, girl?" I asked when she picked up the phone.

"Nothing. Sitting here at work, reading," she said.

"Anything good?" I asked.

"Actually I just finished reading an article that was really good," she replied.

"Is that so? What's the article about?" I asked.

"Dating, and it's actually written by that college poet named Candice we saw at the festival. The article is printed in the local paper. Hang on. Let me find it, because I want to read it to you," Keysha said.

"Okay." Once she found the article, she said, "Okay, listen to this. The article is called 'Just Ask Me Out.' 'While in my organic chemistry class, I had an epiphany about relationships, being single and dating. I myself am a nervous person when it comes to speaking to men. I say the lamest things, like, "Hey, baby, if I were in charge of the alphabet, I'd put *U* and *I* together." Whenever I say that one, dudes glare at me as if I'm psychotic. When guys sweetly say, "Hey, baby," or "How are you doing,

Shorty?" I'm at a complete loss as to how I should respond. Most times I just stand there with a petrified look on my face. I'm sure that every girl on the planet has had something similar happen on at least one occasion.

"'As young adults, we are extremely fickle creatures, whether we like to admit it or not. One day we're crushing over someone we know because we think they're hot and just drop-dead gorgeous. Then, the following day, we've lost interest in that person because someone new has come along. In today's dating world, when that hot guy or girl decides they want to have a conversation, they'll most likely start by following your Twitter posts, where they indirectly get to say whatever they want. This phenomenon is also known as subtweeting.

"'I know from personal experience that relationships can be a drag and highly problematic. No offense to those who are happy in their current courtship. I'm happy for you, and when I see a lovely-looking couple or an ugly couple walking around, I become more optimistic. However, for now, I'm waving the "Team Single" flag. Sometimes, when I'm feeling depressed about being alone, I wish I had a couple of potentials who were interested in a brainy girl who enjoys organic chemistry, and who wouldn't mind a cheap date. Heck, we could even go to the campus cafeteria. I'm not too difficult to please.

"'I believe we all have at least one guy or girl in our phone contact list who is there for us whenever we need a shoulder to cry on, or if we're dealing with a particularly hard professor. However, we place those individuals in the "strictly friends" category because we're too terrified to move forward and nurture a more meaningful and deeper relationship.

"'For all the guys and girls who may happen to read this, I'd like to say that I know it seems like getting to know someone is extremely complicated, but it isn't. Both guys and girls want to be loved, complimented, respected, mentally stimulated and, yes, aroused. There, I said it.

"'If you're single like me, enjoy it and don't be ashamed of your status. Instead, take time learning to love yourself. It's silly to go around telling someone else you love them if you have no clue about how to love yourself. For those of you who have close friends of the opposite sex, please find the courage to ask them out on a date. Chances are pretty strong that they've been waiting for you to do it. Happy dating, and have fun.'"

"Wow. What a great article," I said to Keysha.

"I know. She really nailed it with that one," Keysha agreed.

"Speaking of dating, as much as I don't want to admit this, I have a date this afternoon."

"Great. You finally got Misalo to talk to you?" Keysha asked excitedly.

"No. The date is not with Misalo," I muttered.

"Huh? Please don't tell me you're going out with Carlo," Keysha said.

Instead of giving her a fast no, I gave her a slow yes.

"Maya," Keysha whined.

"I know, but it's not like that, Keysha. I promise you," I explained.

"Girl, you are getting messy," Keysha scolded.

"That's not messy," I fired back because I felt as if I was being attacked.

"Yes, it is. Look, I'm your best friend and I'm going to tell it to you straight. I would've told Carlo no, especially if I were trying to get back with Misalo."

"Keysha, I just felt so bad about what happened. It wasn't fair that he lost his job," I said, trying to find justification for agreeing to have lunch with Carlo.

"He lost his job? When did that happen, and how did you find out?" Keysha was surprised by the news.

"I ran into him at the drugstore earlier. He made me feel guilty, and I figured the least I could do was honor his one request for a simple lunch since Misalo picked a fight with him."

"Maya, that wasn't your fault. You had no idea that Misalo was going to freak out like he did," Keysha replied, pointing out what should've been very clear to me.

"So, you don't think I should go?" I asked.

"I think you're confused right now," Keysha said. I immediately took offense to her comment.

"I'm not confused," I shrieked at her.

"It's okay to be confused," Keysha answered, rephrasing what she'd just said.

"Don't talk to me as if I'm ignorant." I had gotten really upset.

"Maya, calm down. There is no need to raise your voice at me," Keysha said, softening her words.

"You know what? I'm going to go have lunch with Carlo at Pizza Hut. It will only take about an hour. I'm going to tell Carlo that I'm in love with Misalo and that he needs to respect that and stop chasing after me. Then

I'm going to go see Misalo and straighten everything out between us. Even if I have to drop to my knees and wrap my arms around his legs, I'm going to make him listen to me." I felt as if I'd just unloaded on Keysha.

"Okay, I hear you. You're just having lunch to clear up any misunderstandings. I get that. Let me know how everything goes," Keysha replied, backing down. She exhaled.

"As soon as I make up with Misalo, I'll stop by the pool to see you."

"Okay. I'll be here." I could hear Keysha take a sip of something, most likely bottled water, because she always kept some nearby when she was on duty.

"I'll talk to you later," I said and ended the call. I grabbed my purse and checked inside to make sure I had enough money. I then walked over to my door and opened it. Viviana stumbled into my room when the door swung open.

"What the hell!" I snapped at her.

Looking totally surprised, Viviana said, "Oh, I was about to knock on your door."

"For what?" I asked, totally annoyed.

"Your dad wanted me to ask you where you put his sinus medicine."

Looking at Viviana suspiciously, I said, "Oh. I think I left it in the car. I'll go get it for him." Then we both walked toward the staircase.

When I arrived at Pizza Hut, Carlo was already there. He had gotten us a seat and waved for me to come over and join him. I nervously walked toward him and took a seat opposite him.

"I'm so glad you're here. I didn't think you'd make it," he said.

"I didn't think I'd make it, either," I admitted.

"I have a question I've been meaning to ask you." He smiled and leaned forward.

I was almost afraid to ask what his question was, but I found the courage and said, "What do you want to know?"

Before Carlo could answer, a waiter came over and asked to take our order.

"Order whatever you want, Carlo. This one is on me," I said.

"You're sweet," Carlo replied, complimenting me. Carlo ordered a medium pepperoni pizza and two sodas.

The waiter took the order and then left us alone.

"Where was I?" Carlo paused and then snapped his fingers. "Oh, yeah. The night we shared that dance, you know that was very special, right? I felt a great connection between us."

"Carlo." Before I could say anything more, he reached across the table and held my hand.

"Let me finish. I've never met a girl like you before. You're smart, you're fun to be around, and most of all, you're drop-dead gorgeous."

"Did you read the same article that Keysha read?" I asked, because what he was saying sounded just like what Keysha had read.

"I'm not much of a reader, Maya. These words are coming from my heart. Can't you see that?"

At that moment, I didn't know what to do or say. I'd never had to reject anyone before, and for some reason, it wasn't as easy as I thought it would or should be. The waiter returned with our drinks, and I was thankful for the interruption.

"What I'm trying to say, Maya, is that I'd like for you to give me a chance to make you—"

"So, it's true. You've been totally playing me!" Misalo appeared out of nowhere with several guys from the soccer team.

My mouth opened as wide as the sky, but no words would come out. I was both petrified and in shock. I couldn't figure out how he even knew where I was.

"Don't worry. You don't have to say anything. It's over, Maya!" Misalo barked at me.

Tears began falling from my eyes. I wanted to tell him that I loved him and that I was having lunch with Carlo only to tell him to stop pursuing me, but I couldn't, because my words got lodged in my throat.

Rising to his feet, Carlo said, "What the hell is wrong with you, man? You've made her cry!"

Borrowing a line from the movie *New Jack City*, Misalo said, "Sit your five-dollar ass down before I make change! You've disrespected me. I can't let that go." Misalo pointed an angry finger at Carlo.

"What? You want to do something now?" Carlo wasn't about to let Misalo punk him.

"Anytime and anyplace," Misalo said, walking backward and away from us with his friends. "No one disrespects me and gets away with it, Carlo."

"Misalo?" I called.

He cut his eyes at me as if I totally disgusted him. I wanted to explain that my being with Carlo meant nothing.

"Baby," I said sweetly, hoping he'd pause for a minute and allow me to get my thoughts together.

Misalo said nothing as he and his friends walked out, got into his car and drove away.

NINE

VIVIANA

I was in the family room with my Uncle Herman, watching the game show *Jeopardy*. We were having a mini competition to see who could come up with the most right answers to the clues being given. We made a bet that if I won, he had to give me twenty-five dollars. If I lost, I had to do the yard work he was supposed to do. So far, I was kicking his butt and enjoying every minute of it. I had eight hundred points to his six.

"Okay, I'm definitely going to get the next one right," he said confidently as he repositioned himself in his seat. We watched the television and waited for the host to read the next clue. We had agreed that we had to answer in the form of a question before any of the contestants. If we couldn't, we'd have to wait for the next clue. If we both answered at the same time, then we'd both get points. It was a silly little game we were playing, but it was fun and it helped pass the time.

The host said, "For two hundred points, here is the next clue. Archie Bunker's armchair was an integral part of the living room on this classic sitcom."

"All in the Family," Uncle Herman blurted out as he snapped his fingers.

"Who is Archie Bunker?" I lowered my eyebrows and placed a frown on my face.

"He was a character on a seventies television show," Uncle Herman answered.

"Okay. That one was way too easy for you," I griped, but I did remember the answer, in case I ever needed it again.

The host went on to the next clue. "For four hundred points, here is the clue. In the year twelve-seventy-five, Marco Polo visited this city and praised its beauty."

"What is Beijing?" I answered before Uncle Herman could. The contestant on the television repeated the answer I gave, which was correct.

"I didn't know that one," Uncle Herman admitted. "I suppose I should have, but I didn't."

"There are only two clues left, and you need to get both of them right in order to win," I said, feeling my competitive side taking over.

"Here is the next clue, for six hundred points. Hispanic American Lourdes Casal is a writer who is also famous for her studies of this?"

"What are black Cubans?" I leaped out of my seat as I shouted out the answer.

"There is no way you got that one right!" Uncle Herman didn't want to believe that I knew the answer. The clue seemed to stump the contestants on the television. Finally, one of them signaled that he knew the answer.

"They don't know the answer to the clue," Uncle Herman said as he watched the person pause before he gave an answer.

"What are black Cubans?" the contestant said.

"That is correct," said the host.

Tossing my hands in the air, I said, "Yes. Got that one! You might as well give me my money, Uncle Herman." I extended my hand for the cash.

"No. I'm not out just yet. Tell you what. Let's play for double or nothing for the last clue. If I lose, I'll give you fifty bucks." Uncle Herman was such a gung ho man. He couldn't stand losing, especially to me.

"You've got a deal," I said, hoping the last clue wasn't too hard. It was worth the risk to me because fifty bucks would set me straight for a minute.

The host of the show gave the last clue. "Fort Pulaski National Monument is located near this city?"

"What is Chicago?" Uncle Herman blurted out, confident he had the right answer.

"No, I think it's in Georgia somewhere," I said, uncertain of the city in Georgia.

"What is Savannah?" answered one of the contestants.

"Ha-ha, I was right," I said, once again holding out my hand for my cash prize. "Come on. Don't be slow about handing me my winnings." I stood in front of Uncle Herman and did a little happy dance.

He wanted to squabble. "You cheated."

"No, I did not!" I said, not wanting to hear him grumble about losing.

"Do I have to pay you now?" Uncle Herman asked, stalling.

"Don't make me beat you down," I said teasingly.

Uncle Herman stood up, reached for his wallet but then stopped. "I'm going to tickle you," he said out of the clear blue. He made a motion as if he were going to do it, and I flinched and laughed.

"No," I said as I laughed uncontrollably at the thought of being tickled.

"Ha!" Uncle Herman made a tickling motion again, and I fell to the floor like a giddy two-year-old. Playing like this reminded me of when I was a little girl and horsed around with my dad.

"Please, just give me my money," I begged him as I stood back up.

Uncle Herman removed the money from his wallet and held it out to me. Just as I was about to take it, he snatched it back.

"Come on. Stop playing," I said. He turned his back to me and I attempted to reach around him to grab it. I couldn't stop laughing at how silly we were being.

"What's going on here?"

I turned in the direction of the voice and saw that Maya had walked into the family room through the garage.

"Nothing. We're just horsing around," answered Uncle Herman.

"I just beat Uncle Herman at *Jeopardy*," I informed Maya, who wrinkled up her face and looked as if she'd just been sprayed with a can of skunk funk.

"What's wrong with you, Maya? Why are you looking like that?" asked Uncle Herman.

"I've had a rough day, Dad." Maya's sour expression suddenly teetered on the edge of tears.

"Do you want to talk about it?" asked Uncle Herman.

"No. You're playing with her!" Maya said, sounding like a spoiled brat. I glanced at Uncle Herman and shrugged my shoulders, as if I had no idea why she'd flipped out.

"I'm going to go talk to Mom," Maya said and rushed out of the room.

Before Uncle Herman could chase after her, I said, "Have you considered sending her to a psychiatrist for an evaluation?" I tried to sound as if I was joking, but in my heart I wasn't.

"No. Why would I do that?" asked Uncle Herman as he watched Maya hustle up the stairs.

"Seems to me like she has wild mood swings. You know, I've read that people who behave like her might be bipolar. I seriously think you and Aunt Raven should send Maya to a professional to make sure she's working with a full deck, if you know what I mean," I said, tapping my index finger on my temple.

Uncle Herman turned his attention back to me. He glanced at me for a moment and then said, "Maybe I should have *you* evaluated."

"Me!" I exclaimed, raising my voice in protest. "What for?"

"You knew the answers to some rather challenging questions. I think you're much smarter than you're giving yourself credit for. Perhaps you should be tested."

"Oh, God. Please don't do that. I can't stand tests. I just know stuff because I remember everything I hear and I sort of have this photographic-memory thing going on," I admitted.

Placing his right index finger on his right cheek, Uncle

Herman said, "I'm going to talk to Raven about it. I personally think you're smarter than you realize."

When Uncle Herman said that to me, I didn't know why I became emotional. Maybe it was because it had been a long time since anyone had thought or told me I was smart. I wanted to hug him. I wanted to press my face against his chest, wrap my arms around him and wait for him to hug me back. Although I truly wanted to do this, I didn't, because it would probably feel awkward since he and I had never had that type of sentimental relationship. Still, I felt the need to express my gratitude in some way.

I curled my fingers into a fist and extended my arm for a fist bump. "Yeah, Uncle Herman, I am probably the smartest girl on the planet," I proudly boasted.

Uncle Herman returned the fist bump and then said, "Well, here is your money." He handed me my fifty bucks. I quickly took it and counted it.

Laughing, Uncle Herman asked, "What? You don't trust me?"

"Hey, when it comes to my cash, I have got to make sure," I said as I rolled up the five ten-dollar bills he'd given to me.

"I'm going to go check on Maya," Uncle Herman said.

I was cool with that because I'd gotten my cash. I exited the house and was about to find Anna to see what she was up to. The last time I'd seen her, she was in the backyard, blabbing on the phone with one of her girlfriends. As I walked around the house, I received a phone call of my own. I removed my phone and saw that Misalo was calling me.

"Hello?" I answered as a sinister smile spread across my face.

"Yeah, what's up?" He didn't sound very pleased, and I had a good idea why.

"What happened, honey? You don't sound too happy," I said. I wanted Misalo to let his guard down and totally trust me.

"Can you meet me somewhere? I'd like to talk to you," he said.

"Sure. I'm not doing anything. Where you would like to hook up?" I asked.

"Do you know where the community center is?" he asked.

"Yeah. It's near the high school, right?" I asked.

"Yeah. That's the spot. Can you meet me there in about twenty minutes?" he asked.

"Sure. I'll see you then," I said and hung up. I stood still for a moment as I replayed our brief conversation in my mind and tried to analyze what it meant. Then a strange feeling came over me. I suddenly felt as if someone were watching me. I glanced over my shoulder and up at a window of the house. I saw Maya standing in the window, glaring down at me.

"That's creepy," I muttered to myself as I continued on my way.

When I arrived at the community center, Misalo hadn't made it there yet. I walked toward the gym and watched some guys, who looked as if they were college age, play basketball. It was clearly shirts versus skins, and I'm not going to even lie, but they looked like gods. Their bodies were hot, and one guy in particular had a nice butt. I was so caught up with peeping in on the basketball game that I didn't hear Misalo come up behind me. He touched my shoulder, causing me to nearly leap out of my skin.

"I'm sorry. I didn't mean to scare you," he said, apologizing.

Swallowing hard and placing my hand over my heart, I said, "It's okay."

"Come on. Let's sit down," he said and motioned for us to sit on a nearby bench. I let Misalo walk in front of me so that I could sneak a peek at his rear end. He was wearing workout shorts and a tank top. I must admit, his behind looked delicious enough to smack. I also checked out his arms, which, for some reason, seemed bigger than I remembered.

"Are you lifting weights?" I asked.

"Yeah. I've been working on building more muscle," he said as he sat down. I sat next to him and boldly touched his biceps muscle.

"Nice," I said.

"Look, I wanted to thank you for the tip you gave me," he said.

I almost didn't hear him, because I was thinking about what it would feel like to have his arms wrapped around me.

"Viviana, did you hear me?" Misalo snapped me out of my reverie.

"Oh, yeah. No problem, baby. When I overheard Maya talking to Carlo and making plans to meet up, I knew I had to tell you so that you could see with your own eyes how Maya is playing you."

"You know, I didn't want to believe that Maya was like that. I really didn't want to fully believe that she and Carlo were dating behind my back, but after seeing them today at Pizza Hut, there is no way that I could ever believe anything she says." Judging by the look in his eyes, I knew Misalo's feelings were teetering between anger and sorrow.

Confidently moving closer to him, I leaned over and spoke purposefully in his ear. "If I were your girl, you'd never have to worry about me creeping around on you," I said sweetly as I softly caressed his back.

Misalo turned and met my gaze. "Is that what you want?" he asked.

"I want to make you happy. I think you deserve a girl who is trustworthy." I knew that I was stabbing Maya in the back, but I didn't care. In my mind, my actions were undeniably justifiable.

"Don't you think dating me is wrong?" he asked.

I kissed his earlobe. "You're not married and neither am I. You broke up with Maya, didn't you?" I asked, although I knew the answer to the question.

"Yes," he answered.

"Then you're just as single as I am. I don't think there is anything wrong with us dating. Besides, all is fair in love and war." I kissed his earlobe again, then his neck, and placed my hand on his thigh. When Misalo didn't resist my advances, a wicked sense of victory filled my heart. I couldn't wait to flaunt my relationship with him in front of Maya.

ten

Keysha hurried into my room. She was wearing a pretty yellow top, a braided brown belt and a cute white skirt with brown sandals, complete with a matching brown purse. Her hair was freshly braided, and on her ears she wore a pair of the cutest earrings I'd ever seen before.

"Girl, I got here as quickly as I could. What's the big emergency?" Keysha was breathless as she sat and rested her purse on my bed. I'd called her in hysterics and begged her to come over to my house as soon as she got off from work.

"Why are you all dressed up?" I asked, noticing how pretty she looked.

"It's my dad's birthday. Everyone is going to take him out to dinner in about an hour," Keysha said.

"I'm sorry," I said. I felt bad for making her come visit me when she really didn't have the time.

"Don't be sorry. I'm here for you and I always will be," Keysha said.

I sat down at the foot of my bed and placed my face in my hands. "It's all messed up, Keysha. Everything has gone totally wrong, and I don't know what to do. My mom isn't here, and I feel like I'm going crazy." I rose to my feet and began pacing. Keysha stood up, clutched my shoulders and forced me to stop moving.

"Maya, what got messed up?" Keysha asked, genuinely concerned about me.

"Misalo saw me eating with Carlo at Pizza Hut," I said, feeling my words getting lodged in my throat.

"Get out! Are you serious?" Keysha didn't believe I was telling her the truth.

"Yes. I'm very serious. I wouldn't joke about something like this."

"How did he find you?" Keysha asked as she covered her mouth with her hand.

Shrugging my shoulders, I said, "I don't know. He just sort of walked in on us."

"Well, what did you say?" Keysha asked.

"I froze up. I couldn't talk. All I know is that when Misalo left, he looked at me as if he hated my guts." I got choked up, and tears began flowing.

Keysha hugged me as I cried on her shoulder. "Okay. I think we can still fix this," she said, trying to calm me.

"How? I can't even get him to talk to me," I said, pulling away from her before my tears ruined her pretty blouse.

"On my way over here, I walked past the community center and saw Misalo walking in. He looked as if he was going to work out," Keysha said, handing me my sunglasses from the top of my dresser. "Put them on."

"Why?" I asked.

"Because I'm going to help you clear all of this up

today. We're going over to the community center, and you and Misalo are going to stop avoiding each other and talk. You guys just need to work out your problem."

I sniffled as I put on my sunglasses. "You're right," I said. "It's time to stop being so stubborn and go get my man." I exhaled deeply as I moved toward my bedroom door. I stopped in the bathroom briefly just to clean myself up a little.

Keysha followed me. "I don't want to look hideous when he sees me," I said, reaching for a tissue in the bathroom cupboard.

"You look fine," Keysha assured me as I blew my nose.

"Yeah, right." I didn't agree with her.

"Listen to me. Looking a bit unhinged will help you in this situation," Keysha said as she pulled my hair away from my face.

"How?" I asked.

"Because if you look like you're really upset, Misalo will see that you totally love him and he should at least hear your side of the story," Keysha explained.

"What if he doesn't listen? What if he walks away like he has been? It's so unlike him to just turn his back on me," I said, trying to understand his behavior.

"That's because his heart is just as broken as yours. He's just dealing with it differently. Besides, if he doesn't talk to you, he's going to have me to deal with."

What Keysha said made sense to me. "Okay, I'm ready. Let's do this." I swallowed hard before walking out of the bathroom toward my unknown future with Misalo.

When Keysha and I walked through the front door of the community center, we were thankful that the air-conditioning was working, because it was still very hot outside.

"I need some water," Keysha remarked as soon as she spotted the water fountain mounted on a nearby wall. She headed over for a long drink. I glanced around the lobby for signs of Misalo but did not see him.

"Are you sure it was him that you saw?" I asked as I walked over to Keysha.

"Of course I'm sure it was him," Keysha said as she tucked one of her long braids behind her ear. "He's around here someplace."

"Let me check the basketball court." I walked over to the gym doors and peeked inside. All I saw were some college age guys shooting hoops. I turned to Keysha and said, "He's not in there."

"When he works out, what does he usually do?" Keysha asked.

I thought about the last time I saw Misalo at the gym and remembered that he'd been on this kick to build muscle. Snapping my fingers, I said, "The weight room. He's probably in there."

Keysha and I walked up a flight of stairs to the second floor and entered the weight room. We walked around the room but did not find him.

"Where the heck could he be?" Keysha said aloud.

"Well, let's check the indoor track. Maybe he's there jogging around or something," I suggested.

"I hope so, because the only place left would be the men's locker room and I'm not going in there to look for him," Keysha said jokingly. As we left the weight room, Keysha couldn't help but notice a good-looking guy who was flexing his muscles in a mirror. "He's cute." Keysha pointed to the guy who'd caught her eye.

Slightly irritated, I said, "Can we focus on finding Misalo?"

"Don't get mad. He was cute. And I could see myself enjoying the feel of his arms wrapped around me." Keysha chuckled.

We walked down a corridor toward a section of the gym where there were televisions, small sofas and bar stools and people could relax and kill time. As we approached that area, I stopped. My eyes narrowed to slits as I focused on Misalo sitting on a stool, sipping a drink he'd probably gotten from one of the vending machines. Leaning over him from behind was Viviana. She had her hands inside his shirt and was rubbing his chest. Her cheek was pressed against his, and I didn't like it one bit.

"What the hell is this?" I blurted out.

"What?" Keysha asked, startled by the change in the tone of my voice.

"Them!" I pointed in the direction of Viviana and Misalo. Keysha had to move slightly to her right in order to see them because a vending machine against the wall blocked her view.

"Oh, wow!" Keysha said as I rushed toward them to find out why my cousin was all up on my man.

"What the hell is this about, Misalo?" I said, shoving Viviana away from him.

"Oh, you've got some nerve! I've busted you three times with another guy," Misalo yelled as he rose to his feet.

"You wouldn't even give me a chance to explain my side of the damn story!" I screamed.

Raising his voice to an equally aggressive level, Misalo said, "You have no story to explain, Maya. I've seen you with my own eyes."

"You haven't seen anything, Misalo!" I shouted as my emotions took over.

"I've seen enough, Maya," he growled as he started walking away from me.

"No. You can't walk away from this!" I rushed around to stand in front of him.

Viviana interjected, "Maya, you just need to let him go. He's done with you!"

Viviana ticked me off. I turned around slowly and gave her an evil glare that would have made the devil jump with fear. "First of all, you need to stay out of my damn business!" I pointed my finger at her.

"Excuse me, but in case you didn't notice, you were in *my* business. Misalo and I were doing just fine until your loudmouthed butt showed up with this mutt you call a friend," Viviana retorted.

"Oh, hell no. You need to watch who you're calling a mutt!" Keysha stormed.

I knew Keysha wasn't going to allow Viviana to insult her and get away with it. I momentarily glanced around at the other people in this section of the community center. They had stunned expressions on their faces. They all watched and waited to see the outcome of the argument.

"You don't have any business with Misalo!" I exclaimed, raising my voice again at Viviana.

"Maya, you need to go find Carlo. That's who you really want," Misalo said.

I turned back to him. His words hurt me so badly. I

felt my breath escaping me. "Is that what you think?" I said, tearing up.

"It doesn't matter what I think, because you say one thing, Maya, and do another," Misalo said, completely believing that I'd done something wrong.

"I've done nothing wrong!" I responded, pleading with him to believe me.

"You shouldn't believe a word she's saying. Maya has always been a sneaky liar," Viviana boldly announced.

I stopped restraining myself and lunged for her. I tried to grab a fistful of her hair so that I could sling her to the floor and punch her until my arms got tired. Viviana quickly moved out of the way. I began swinging my arms wildly at her, hoping to land a punch. Viviana easily maneuvered around my fist windmill, grabbed my hair and punched the side of my face. I screamed and cursed her as she continually punched me in the jaw. She slung me to the floor and got on top of me.

"Damn! Move, Misalo!" I heard Keysha shout.

The next thing I knew, Viviana was being pulled off of me by Keysha. Keysha slammed Viviana against a wall. Viviana grabbed Keysha's blouse and ripped it at the shoulder. Keysha nailed Viviana with a fist to the mouth. Viviana began clawing at Keysha's face and neck. Viviana then grabbed hold of Keysha's hair and pulled it so hard that one of her braids came out.

"Oh, no, you didn't pull my damn hair!" Keysha barked at Viviana as she once again slammed her back and head against the wall, knocking the wind of out Viviana.

"Come on. Stop it!" Misalo finally stepped between Viviana and Keysha.

"You need to stay out of my business!" Viviana said as she released Keysha's hair. "I'm not done with you yet, either!" Viviana pointed her finger at me as Misalo pushed her away from us. He was heading toward the door.

"Misalo, you need to realize that I love you!" I said tearfully.

I was about to chase after him but stopped when I heard Keysha say, "I can't believe she ruined my outfit and messed up my hair."

I turned toward my best friend, who'd gotten into a fight for me. I felt horrible. I could see red claw marks on her cheek and neck where Viviana had scratched her. Keysha's blouse was ripped, and part of her bra was exposed.

"I'm so sorry," I said as my legs buckled beneath me. I crumpled to the floor and began sobbing uncontrollably.

I thought for sure Keysha would be so pissed off with me for starting a fight and forcing her to get involved that she'd walk away and leave me there. Keysha said nothing. She helped me to my feet, and we walked out the door, battered and bruised, before the authorities could arrive and ask a bunch of questions that I didn't want to answer.

Eleven

VIVIANA

Misalo offered to drive me home. I happily accepted his offer because I didn't want to walk down the street, looking like a victim of mob violence. As soon as I sat in the passenger seat, I flipped down the sun visor and took a look at my face in the small mirror. Keysha had landed a lucky shot on my mouth and had split my bottom lip. She'd also landed a shot just below my left eye. The area was all red and swollen. I knew that it was going to turn into a nasty-looking bruise. I felt the back of my head and found a small lump from where my head had smashed into the wall. Once we were situated, Misalo fired up the car and drove away. I wanted him to say something, but he didn't. I wanted to know what he was thinking and how he was feeling, but he wasn't letting me in. The silence in the car became too loud for me, so I decided I should speak.

"Are you mad at me?" I asked.

Misalo remained silent as he adjusted the rearview mirror.

"What did I do?" I asked.

After another long pause, Misalo finally spoke. "I'm mad about a lot of things," he admitted.

"Well, let's start with why you're mad at me." My bottom lip quivered out of nervousness. In my heart, I didn't want him to reject me. Especially not after what I'd just gone through.

"I'm not mad at you," he said. "I'm mad at the way things have turned out."

Breathing a sigh of relief, I said, "Well, I just fought two girls for you. If that doesn't prove how loyal I am, I don't know what will."

Misalo pulled into my driveway and stopped the car. "I know. You certainly have proven yourself to be much more loyal than I thought Maya was." His head slumped between his shoulders. I reached over and stroked his hair. He welcomed my touch briefly and then pulled away. "Look, I need time to clear my head."

"Okay, I understand," I whispered as I stopped touching him. "Will you ever call me again?"

He glanced out the driver's side window. I tried to figure out what he was looking at, but then realized he was avoiding eye contact as he considered how to answer my question. He then met my gaze and said, "Yes."

I wanted to kiss him, if only on the cheek, but my bottom lip was throbbing and bloody. I knew that I didn't exactly look pretty and didn't want to gross him out with a bloody kiss. I opened the door and stepped out of the car. I stood in the driveway and watched as Misalo backed out and drove away.

I walked into the house and heard Uncle Herman and Aunt Raven in the basement laughing. Judging by the sound coming from the television, they were watching some type of comedy program. I hurried up to the room I shared with Anna so that I could hide my battle scars. When I entered the room, Anna was on her bed, resting on her stomach and screwing around with an iPad.

When she saw my face, she said, "What happened to you?" She set the tablet aside and came near me. I tried to hide my face out of shame, but it was no use. "Did you get into a fight?" She asked a question that she already knew the answer to.

"Yeah. It was two against one," I said as I once again surveyed my bruises and cuts in the mirror on top of the dresser. Somehow, either Keysha or Maya had managed to scratch the tip of my nose.

"Let me see your face," Anna insisted.

"It's not that bad. You should see the other girls," I proudly boasted.

"Wow. I can't believe you beat up two girls." Anna seemed to be impressed with me.

"Well, sometimes you just have to do what you have to. I wasn't about to let two chicks jump me," I said.

"Come on. Let's go down the hall and into the bathroom. I'll help bandage you up," Anna offered. I looked at her and gave her a big hug. Anna hugged me back, and I didn't want to let her go.

"You're such a cool cousin," I said, finally releasing her.

"Who did you get into a fight with? I want to know all the details." Anna was adamant as she took my hand and led me out of her room. We entered the bathroom, and she locked the door. She closed the lid on the toilet seat and said, "Take a seat." She opened up the medicine cabinet and removed a first-aid kit.

I remained silent. "Come on, spill it. Who did you fight with?" she asked, pressing me for information.

I exhaled because I didn't want to tell Anna out of fear of how she might react. "It's a long story, Anna."

"Oh, come on. Don't do me like that. Please tell me." She wanted information and wouldn't stop questioning me until she got it. Anna opened a bag of gauze, pressed it against my split bottom lip and cleaned up the blood that was there.

"Do you think I'm going to need stitches?" I asked nervously.

"No, it looks worse than it is. Some A+D Ointment should heal this up just fine. I use it all the time during the winter months, when my bottom lip splits from being chapped. Now, stop stalling and tell me what happened."

"I beat up Maya and her friend Keysha." I finally told her what she wanted to know.

"You did what?" Ann shouted.

"Shhhh, I don't want your parents to know."

"Oh, I'm sorry."

"Are you mad at me?" I asked, fearing the worst.

"Mad at you? No. Maya probably deserved it," Anna said.

"Well, she did start it. She was the one who hit me first," I said.

"See. So it was self-defense, right?" Anna asked.

"It was totally self-defense," I assured her.

She continued with her questioning. "So, what were you guys fighting about?"

"I was at the community center, talking to Misalo, when she and Keysha just showed up. Maya started going off on me and Misalo for no reason other than pure jealousy. She shoved me, and I decided to let the first push go unanswered. Misalo told her that he didn't want to see her anymore. She got very upset with his decision. I was trying to avoid a nasty scene, so I suggested to Misalo that he come with me. Next thing I knew, Maya just snapped off. She began swinging wildly at me. So I beat her down. I slung her to the floor, held her down and started punching her. Next thing I knew, Keysha jumped in and we started fighting."

"Damn! That wasn't right for Keysha to jump in a fight between you and Maya," Anna said, taking my side. I felt relieved that she thought my actions were justified.

"Only problem is that I don't want your parents to know that I beat her up," I said, concerned about the consequences of that discovery.

"Why?" Anna asked.

"Because I don't want them to get so ticked off that they kick me out of the house. I've gotten used to staying here. I don't have to worry about where my next meal is going to come from, and I really like Uncle Herman. I don't want to disappoint him."

"Okay," Anna said as she applied some ointment to my lip. "Do you want me to help?"

"How are you going to help, Anna?" I asked, not convinced she could do anything.

"I'll talk to Maya and tell her that you want to offer a truce," she explained.

"I don't think she'll go for that. She seems like the dramatic type that's going to walk through the front door any minute now, crying as if she's just been shot," I said, fearing the other shoe would drop at any moment.

"Let me find out where she is, and I'll talk to her before she comes into the house," Anna said.

"Do you really think you can get her to just let this go? I mean, I really kicked her butt, Anna." I had my doubts.

"You just leave Maya to me. But you have to promise me that once I set up the truce, you guys will be cool and just stay out of each other's way."

"Trust me. I don't want to be bothered with her any more than she wants to deal with me."

"Cool. Sit tight. I'm going to go get my cell phone and call her," Anna said as she exited the bathroom.

Several minutes later, Anna came back. By that time, I was standing in front of the mirror, trying to apply some makeup to hide the bruise that was forming under my eye.

"So, what's the deal?" I asked.

"She's at Keysha's house right now. I told her that I really needed to talk to her and that I was on my way over."

"She didn't try to blow you off?" I asked.

"Of course she did, but I'm going over there, anyway. Trust me, I'm going to make her an offer she can't refuse," Anna said lightheartedly.

"You've been watching too many mobster movies," I said, knowing Anna enjoyed watching classic movies like *The Godfather* and *Goodfellas* just as much as I did.

"I left my iPad on the bed. You can fiddle around with it until I get back. I've downloaded a few really cool fashion apps." Anna placed her hand on my shoulder. I turned and hugged her once again.

"Have you downloaded any science, math or music programs?" I asked as I walked back into the bedroom and picked up the device.

"Huh?" I'd completely confused Anna with my odd question.

"Okay, so I'm a little bit of a closet geek. I like knowing how stuff works. Do you have a problem with that?" I asked.

Laughing, Anna said, "Not at all. I just never thought you'd be the type of person who was interested in those sorts of things."

"Well, surprise. There is more to me than meets the eye," I said.

"I see," Anna said as she stepped over to the door. Smiling over her shoulder at me, she added, "Everything is going to be okay."

"I hope so," I said, sitting down on the bed.

Anna walked out and closed the door gently.

twelve

MAYA

Keysha and I left the community center and walked back to her house, looking like we'd just left a *Smack-Down* prime-time event. During the scuffle, not only did Keysha's blouse get ripped, but the straps on her sandals had popped, as well. Although I tried not to, I cried on her shoulder during the entire walk to her house. Keysha tried to console me and I did try to listen, but I couldn't bring myself to stop sobbing.

"I know you don't want to hear this, but as your best friend, I think I should tell you," Keysha said once we had turned the corner and were headed down the street her house was on.

"Tell me what?" I asked through my sobs.

"You have to let Misalo go." Although Keysha's words weren't welcomed, they were the truth.

"I'm not ready to let him go, Keysha. I just can't turn my feelings off for him like that." My wounded heart was speaking for me instead of my common sense.

She tried to reason with me. "I know that, but you've got to try. It may be time to move on. I mean, if it's meant to work out, then it will."

Stubbornly, I responded by saying, "I will not lose Misalo to Viviana. That is the ultimate insult."

"I'm not saying it's going to be easy, but we can't keep going around trying to beat her up," Keysha replied, imploring me to think rationally.

We entered her house and walked up the steps and into her family room. Her half brother, Mike, was sitting on the sofa, playing a football game on his Sony PlayStation with a guy who was on our high school football team. When he glanced up at us, he said, "Damn! What happened to your face, Maya?"

"Leave her alone, Mike," Keysha scolded as she guided me through to the kitchen.

"Both of y'all look like y'all got your butts whipped!" Mike blurted out.

"Hey, Maya, I saw those photos you took. They were hot, girl," his friend remarked.

"Don't pay that insensitive jerk any attention," Keysha said as she covered my ears.

"Hey, Mom and Dad will be here soon. So you'd better be ready to go by then. I hope you haven't forgotten about Dad's birthday," Mike shouted.

"You just worry about being ready," Keysha shouted back.

I followed Keysha up the stairs and into the bathroom. I sat on the edge of the bathtub, cupped my hands and buried my face.

"I can't believe that girl scratched up my face," Keysha complained as she studied herself in the mirror.

At that moment, I felt my cell phone vibrating.

"Who is that calling you?" Keysha asked.

"It's my little sister, Anna," I said, glancing at the caller ID.

"Well, see what she wants," Keysha said as I answered my phone.

"Hello," I answered tearfully.

"Hey. Where are you at?" Anna asked.

"With Keysha at her house," I said.

"Okay. I'm on my way over. I need to talk to you."

"What for?" I asked, suddenly becoming irritated by her forcefulness.

Anna was direct and to the point. "Because we need to talk about the fight you had today."

"What about it?" I asked, snarling at the thought of Viviana.

"When I get there, we'll talk," Anna said and hung up the phone.

"What was that about?" Keysha asked as she removed a face towel from the cupboard. She ran some cool water on it, wrung out the excess water and lightly dabbed her face. "Dang it, my face feels like it's on fire. Viviana must have some seriously sharp nails," Keysha griped.

"I'm so sorry that I dragged you into this mess." I rose to my feet and approached her. "I'll pay for your blouse and some new shoes," I said, glancing at my face in the mirror for the first time. "Damn, what did she do to me?" My entire face was swollen from the vicious blows that Viviana had dished out.

"You're going to have to put a cold compress on your face to help the swelling go down," Keysha informed me.

"My eyes are so puffy." I was utterly disgusted at the sight of my face.

"I honestly believe most of the swelling is from you crying," Keysha said as she opened a drawer and removed a tube of antibiotic ointment to apply to the scratch marks on her face and neck.

"That's okay. When I see her again, I'm going to get even with her," I proclaimed as my loathing of her began to rise again.

"You need to leave her alone," Keysha said. "That girl knows how to fight. I haven't been in a scrap like that in a long time. I just know I'm going to feel all kinds of body aches later on."

"I'll have something for her next time," I said, allowing my battered ego to speak for me.

"I don't want you getting into any more fights that you can't win," Keysha scolded. "OMG. I sound like my grandmother Katie." Keysha shivered at the thought of sounding like an adult. "What are your folks going to say when they find out you picked a fight with your cousin?" Keysha asked.

I sat back down on the edge of the tub, exhaled and once again buried my face in my hands. "They're going to want to kill me for trying to beat her up."

"Well, what they don't know won't really hurt them, now, will it?" I heard my little sister, Anna, say. When I popped my head up, Anna was standing in the doorway.

"How did you get up here?" Keysha asked.

"Your brother, Mike, let me in," Anna said, then looked at me. "Dang! Viviana kicked your butt, Maya."

"No, she didn't," I snapped at Anna. "What do you want, anyway? Why did you come over here?"

"To talk about the terms of the truce between you and

Viviana," Anna said as she closed the lid on the toilet seat and sat down.

"Oh, no! We're still at war!" I said, waving my finger disapprovingly.

"Look, you need to just calm down," Anna said, trying to reason with me.

I was about to get really nasty with her when Keysha said, "I think you should at least hear your little sister out, Maya."

"Fine," I said and folded my arms.

"Okay. Viviana is willing to stay out of your way just as long as you stay out of hers."

"Yeah, she needs to stay out of my way and out of my business," I said.

Anna went on. "About your business with Misalo. As long as you don't mess with Viviana, I'll keep my mouth shut about how you're the one who started the fight and about you secretly creeping around with Misalo against our parents' wishes."

"I'm not going to let her take my boyfriend!" I yelled at her.

"Wow! I was hoping that I wouldn't have to go there, but you're being stubborn as usual," Anna said.

"How does protecting my relationship with my boyfriend equate to being stubborn?" I asked.

"Let me put it to you this way. As long as you stay out of her way, I won't tell Mom and Dad about the photos you took for Misalo that are floating around the neighborhood."

I opened my mouth to say something and then shut it. I didn't know what to say.

"Sounds to me like we have an agreement, right?" Anna asked.

I couldn't bring myself to say anything. My heart was so confused and broken. I still hadn't gotten to the bottom of why Misalo had forwarded the photos when he told me he had deleted them.

Keysha spoke for me. "Anna, she agrees."

"I want to hear her say it," Anna replied, pressing the issue.

I met her gaze for a moment, then nodded my head in agreement.

"Cool," Anna said, rising to her feet. "I'll let Viviana know that you've accepted the truce and that as long as you guys stay out of each other's way, everything will be fine. I'll see you when you get home." On that note Anna left.

"I know what you're thinking, Maya," Keysha said.

"No, you don't," I told her.

"Yes, I do. You're still looking for answers and closure, and until you find out why Misalo did what he did, you won't be happy."

I looked into my friend's eyes as my tears once again surfaced. "You're right. What he did to me was wrong, and the least he could do is explain to me why he decided to ruin our relationship."

"You know, maybe that's why he's been avoiding you. Maybe that's why he's been blaming you for everything. Maybe he doesn't want to admit that he was a real bastard for forwarding the pictures. If he wanted to break up with you, he could've just been man enough to come to you and tell you, instead of humiliating you."

"You're right, Keysha. I don't know if he'll ever own up to his part in all of this. I think it's time for me to realize that it's over between us."

"I know it's not going to be easy." Keysha came and sat beside me. "I'm here for you if you need me."

"Thanks," I said as I looked at her hair. "Let me help you put the braid back."

"Is it noticeable?" Keysha asked, touching the back of her head where Viviana had yanked out her hair.

"Yeah, it's noticeable," I said, taking a closer look.

"Damn," Keysha griped.

"I can fix it," I assured her. I rose to my feet and pulled her up. "Come on. Let me do this and get out of your house before your parents come home. Do you have any more of the hair that was used?"

"Yes. It's in my bedroom. But before we get started, let's take care of your face with a cold compress so that at least some of the swelling can go down. There are ice packs downstairs in the freezer," Keysha said as she opened the cupboard and pulled down a fresh towel.

"You're such a good friend." I gave her a hug and held on to her.

"The best in the world," she answered as she returned the hug.

thirteen

I'd be the first to admit that sometimes I get very depressed. If my father were still around, he'd cheer me up. He was the type of dad who would always make me smile, laugh and feel good about myself. I was his little angel and he was my protector. My dad was also a very smart man. He told me that when he was a student, he was the smartest kid at his school and all his teachers adored him. When he was a fifth grader, he scored very high on the state standardized test. He was only a few points away from a perfect grade. The principal at his school congratulated him by making an announcement of his achievement. A letter was even sent to his home, saying that my father was a gifted student. Although his parents loved the good news, my father said he hated it because it marked the start of bullying by boys in sixth and seventh grade who enjoyed beating up boys like him who were smart.

I asked my father how he'd become so smart, and he said, "I don't know, Viviana. I was just the kind of kid who absorbed everything. If someone showed me how to do something once, I could remember. My brain was like a computer. Once the information was plugged in, it stayed there." I remembered telling him that I wanted my brain to be like a computer. When he told me this, I was a fourth grader. I remembered thinking that I wanted to score well on the standardized test just as he had. I wanted to make him proud of me and to be smart like him.

Anna, Aunt Raven and Maya had gone out to run errands. They were going to Bed Bath & Beyond and to Target to do some shopping. Aunt Raven had invited me to come along, but I had refused to go. The last person I wanted to be near was Maya. After our fight, we'd both agreed to stay out of each other's way. We had a truce—if I didn't bother her, then she wouldn't bother me. I was fine with this arrangement for now, but my gut feeling told me the truce wouldn't last for very long. I just knew that someway, somehow, Maya would do something to irritate me and we'd be feuding again.

Since Maya and Anna were out of the house, I passed the time by goofing around with Anna's iPad. It was actually her dad's old iPad, because he'd gotten an updated one. Anna was the only one in the house who had wanted the old one, so Uncle Herman gave it to her. Anna told me I could use it anytime. Out of all the cool apps I could've downloaded, I chose to download educational stuff. I downloaded an app on the Aztec Empire and one for Scrabble. Just to excite the geek in me, I downloaded a spelling app.

Forty-five minutes passed, and I was totally into my Scrabble game. The last thing I expected to get was a phone call from Misalo. When I saw his name flash across the caller ID, I immediately answered the phone.

"Hello?" I said and then held my breath. I didn't know what to say or what was going to happen next.

"Viviana?" he asked, just to make sure he was actually speaking to me.

"Yes," I answered and said no more.

"Are you busy right now?" he asked.

"No," I said as I placed the iPad on the bed next to me.

"Would you like to go out and get something to eat with me?" he asked.

"Yes," I answered. I feared that if I said too much, he'd change his mind.

"Can you be ready in about a half hour?" he asked.

"Okay," I said and held my breath once more.

"Why don't you walk down to the corner of the street that you live on? I'm driving and can pick you up from there," he said.

"You don't want to pick me up at the house?" I asked, thinking that he did not want Maya to see us together. I knew she'd probably be back by the time Misalo would be driving up to get me. I, on the other hand, wanted her to know that he was picking me up.

"It's not that. Maya's dad doesn't like me too much, and I don't want to cause any trouble with him," he stated.

"Oh, okay. I understand," I said.

"I knew you would. I'll see you shortly," Misalo said and hung up the phone.

I began scrambling for something decent to wear. I searched through all my clothes, and nothing I owned was even remotely appealing. I wanted to look fabulous for Misalo. I wanted him to see a beautiful girl that he could adore and cherish. I knew Anna wouldn't mind if I raided her closet, so I did. I found one decent outfit, but it wasn't my size. Anna was much taller and slimmer than I was. Just as I was about to give up on the idea of looking marvelous for Misalo, a wicked thought came to mind. I said to myself, *Maya will never know if I raid her closet. She already has a ton of outfits and probably won't miss one.*

With that in mind, I gave myself permission to enter Maya's space and rifle through her closet for something decent. Maya and I didn't have the same taste in clothing, but I was so willing to overlook that. To my delight, I located a black T-shirt with two bands of brown and blue on the front. The top still had the price tag on it, which meant that Maya hadn't even worn it yet. I told myself that she'd probably forgotten that she even had it. I went into another closet of hers and began searching for some jeans to wear. Maya and I both wore the same size jeans. As I searched deep into her closet, I found four pairs of jeans, all of which still had tags on them.

"This is just ridiculous," I mumbled to myself. I found it downright appalling that Maya had more clothes than she could possibly wear. I snatched all four pairs of jeans and headed toward the room I shared with Anna. I tried on all of them and settled on the pair that didn't make my butt look too big or too small. I then searched through the makeup Anna had on her dresser so I could mask any unsightly scratches that were visible from the fight I'd had with Keysha and Maya. I'd noticed earlier that Maya had done a pretty good job of hiding her bruises before she went out with her mother and Anna. I took what I needed from Anna's dresser, grabbed the top and headed toward the bathroom to freshen up.

Once I was dressed and my hair was fixed decently, I went back into Anna's room and found some perfume called Wonderstruck, by Taylor Swift. I liked the scent, so I squirted a little on my neck. I took another quick look at myself in the mirror. "Well, I don't look perfect, but it will have to do," I said to my reflection.

I told Uncle Herman, who was in the basement, trying to unclog the sink down there, that I was making a quick run to the store for some personal items. I hated to lie to him, but I didn't want to chance him asking for more details than necessary. Lucky for me, Uncle Herman's attention was focused on breaking up the clog in the drain and not on me. Once I was out of the house, I walked as fast as I could without actually running to the rendezvous point with Misalo. I arrived just as he pulled up. I got in the car, got situated and sat nervously as he whisked me away.

Misalo quickly glanced over at me and said, "You look very nice."

"Thank you," I said, feeling butterflies dancing in my tummy.

"What do you want to eat?" he asked.

"I don't know. Whatever you want," I said, wanting to be as easygoing as possible. I didn't want him to think for one second that I was one of those difficult-to-deal-with girls.

"Why don't we go to Chili's?" suggested Misalo.

"I'd like that," I replied as I looked at him. I tried hard not to stare at him, but I couldn't help it. He really was a very cute guy. "So, what made you want to call me?" I asked. I needed and wanted to know what he was thinking.

Misalo shrugged his shoulders and remained silent for a brief moment before saying what was on his mind. "I have decided to let Maya go. In my mind, she's clearly seeing another guy."

Feeling wicked, I said, "I've been telling you that for how long now?"

"I have a thick skull." Misalo glanced over at me and smiled.

I smiled back at him, feeling as if I'd won the prize of the century.

We arrived at Chili's. Misalo parked the car and we walked in. When we walked in the door, my ears immediately picked up on an old Phil Collins song called "In the Air Tonight." We'd walked in on the part where the drum solo kicked in. Misalo heard it as well, and he began moving his hands as if he were actually playing the drum solo.

"I love this song," he said as the hostess greeted us.

"How many in your party?" she asked.

"Two," Misalo answered.

The hostess took two menus from a nearby countertop and directed us to follow her. She tried to seat us at a table, but I asked if we could sit in a nearby booth instead.

"Sure," she answered and placed the menus on the table I'd pointed out to her.

Once the hostess left, I decided it was time to make my move and be very bold. I wanted Misalo to know that I wanted to belong to him. Instead of sitting opposite him in the booth, I sat directly beside him. "I hope you don't mind," I said as I turned my head and looked into his eyes.

Smiling sweetly, Misalo answered, "I don't mind if you don't."

"Good." I relaxed.

Misalo picked up a menu and began looking at it. Instead of picking up my own to glance at, I snuggled closer to him. Being very forward, I lifted his right arm and rested my head on his shoulder so we could read the menu together.

"What are you going to have?" I asked.

"I love their nachos." Misalo pointed it out on the menu. "What about you? What are you going to have?"

"The chicken fajitas look pretty good." I pointed to the picture on the menu.

"Yeah, I've had those before. They're pretty good," Misalo proclaimed.

"You can have some of mine if you'd like," I said, feeling the electricity of romance flowing through me. Having Misalo's arm draped over me felt wonderful.

"You smell very pretty," he said, complimenting me.

A smile spread across my face as wide as the horizon. "Thank you, boo," I whispered, snuggling even closer to him.

"How are you healing up?" he asked.

I wanted to snap at him and say, "Oh, now you want to show some concern for me after the fact." Instead of causing him to get defensive, I twisted things a little and said, "I hope I've finally proven myself to you once and for all."

"Yes, you have. I've never seen a girl who fights as

well as you. Where did you learn how to throw down like that?" he asked.

"My dad," I said.

Misalo chuckled. "Man, your father must've been one heck of a guy. It sounds like he taught you a lot of survival skills."

"Yeah, he was the type of man who wanted me to be able to defend myself. At one point in his life, he was an amateur boxer," I explained.

"Really?" Misalo seemed excited about what I'd just shared.

"Yeah, he was tough. He got into boxing because he wanted to learn how to protect himself from bullies at school." I continued to tell the story my father had shared with me.

"Is that right?" Misalo seemed genuinely interested in what I was telling him about my dad. I loved the fact that he listened. I decided to reposition my body and sit upright.

"Yes. My father told me the older kids were always picking on him because he was smart. Then one day, while walking home from school, a group of older boys chased him down an alley. When they caught him, they backed him up against a chain-link fence and used his body for their punching bag. Once they were done with him, he was pretty banged up. He told me that he had to force himself to stop crying about being jumped. He sucked up his pain, gathered his things and started heading home.

"He told me that on his way back, he walked past a fire station. One of the firefighters who was pulling down the

American flag from the flagpole noticed my dad's injuries and asked him what happened. My dad talked to the guy, who was nice enough to get a first-aid kit and patch him up. After hearing the explanation my dad gave, the firefighter suggested that he go to a nearby boxing gym. My dad followed the advice and began taking boxing lessons. He was only about eleven at the time, but he told me that boxing quickly became something he fell in love with."

"Did he ever go pro?" Misalo asked.

"No, but by the time he was seventeen years old, he had an impressive record and was given the opportunity to fight the number-one Golden Gloves contender for the Chicago area. My dad went the distance with the guy, but he lost the fight according to the decision of the judges."

"Well, did he get a rematch?" Misalo asked excitedly.

"I don't know. My dad never told me what happened after that or why he stopped boxing. Since he never said any more about it, I didn't, either," I explained. At that moment, I wished he were there so that I could ask him about it.

"So, like, what kind of boxing stuff did your dad teach you?" Misalo asked as he repositioned himself and leaned his back against the windowsill.

"General stuff, like how to throw my hands, how to move and how to avoid a punch," I revealed.

"What about combinations? Did he teach you how to put together some good combination shots?" Misalo balled up his hands and punched the air.

"Yes," I said, giggling at how silly he looked.

"Give me an example of one," he said, insisting that I show him.

"No. I'm not going to stand up in the middle of this restaurant and give you boxing lessons." I laughed out loud.

"Just show me something really quick while you're sitting here," he pleaded with me. I paused for a moment as I thought about a lesson my father had given me about combination punches.

"Okay," I said, sitting up straighter. "The jab is the most important punch in boxing. It will help you in your defense and your offense."

"Like this?" Misalo simulated a jab, but his punch was wild and uncoordinated.

"No. If you punch an opponent like that, you're just asking to get knocked on your butt," I said.

Laughing as if he were mocking me, Misalo said, "What was wrong with my punch?"

"Well, first of all, you're sitting down, and throwing a jab has a lot to do with your stance, as well as hand movement." I figured I could show him better than I could tell him, so I said, "Pay attention. You want to be loose when you throw a punch. You don't want your shoulders and back to be tight. If you're tight, you're burning needless energy. You have to hold your arms up so that your forearms are near your chest. You want snapping power with your jab. So, when you extend your arm, you'll want to rotate your fist so that you thumb corkscrews toward the ground. When you do this, your shoulder will automatically rotate into your chin, protecting it from a counterpunch." I demonstrated it slowly so he could see what I was talking about.

"Oh, how cool." I could tell that Misalo was absorbing

everything I was teaching him. "I want to learn every-thing that you know about boxing," Misalo said, clearly impressed.

"I only know general stuff. I'm no expert," I said, laughing.

"That's okay. You still know more than I do. I think it's so cool that you know how to box. You remind me of that movie that was out not too long ago about the girl who wanted to be a prizefighter."

"I'm no prizefighter," I said, unsure of how to take his comment.

"I know that. You're more like a gangster girl. You'd have my back if we were ever out anywhere and had to throw down." Misalo smiled at me.

I didn't know how to take his comment. I didn't know if I should be happy that he thought I was a gangster girl or offended.

Misalo noticed the confused expression on my face and clarified what he meant. "If I ever got into trouble, Maya would either cry like a baby or run like a coward. You, on the other hand, would knock someone out," Misalo proudly said.

"So, do you like girls like that?" I asked, wanting to be certain I was the type of chick he liked.

"Yes. A Latina like you is a rare find," he proudly said.

"Does this mean I'm better than Maya?" I asked.

Scratching the side of his neck, Misalo said, "You're certainly completely different from Maya." I interpreted his response to mean I was much better than Maya could ever hope to be, and that made me glow.

"Would you give me private lessons?" Misalo asked.

In my mind I said to myself, *I'll give you anything you want.* I certainly wasn't going to tell him exactly what I was thinking.

"Sure," I answered, thinking about how romantic it was going to be spending time with him.

"Aren't you going to ask me why I want to know how to box?" Misalo seemed disappointed that I hadn't inquired.

"I just figured you were curious, that's all," I said, not wanting to seem as if I wasn't in sync with his thoughts and feelings.

"No. I've been hearing rumors that Carlo wants to kick my butt." Misalo picked up a glass of water that was on the table and took a sip.

"Really? Why?" I asked, suddenly feeling concern for his safety.

"He's ticked off about losing his job and is blaming me for it." Misalo met my gaze for a moment before taking another sip of water.

"Why doesn't he just let that go?" I asked, feeling my heart rate increase.

"If I were him, I wouldn't let it go." I could tell Misalo's ego was getting in the way of common sense.

"When are you going to fight him?" I asked.

"I don't know. I could be anywhere and run into him, so I need to be prepared for anything."

"Misalo, I don't like that," I admitted, feeling very uncomfortable.

"It is what it is, you know. Whatever is going to happen will happen. There is nothing I can do about that."

I reached over and brushed the back of my hand down

the curve of his cheek. His skin was smooth and soft. Misalo didn't have much facial hair, which was appealing. "I don't want to see your face all bloody and bruised," I said, genuinely concerned.

"Then you'd better teach me well," he said, as if I had all the answers to his problems with Carlo.

"Maybe you should find a boxing gym or a martial arts instructor. Maybe it would be better if you learned from a guy," I said, suddenly feeling unsure of what I could teach him.

"Yeah, I thought about that, too, but my folks can't afford to pay for martial arts lessons, so I just have to make do." Misalo sounded so disappointed.

"What about other guy friends? I'm sure you could learn some stuff from them," I suggested.

"I've asked them, as well. So, between all my friends and you, I should know enough to beat Carlo down." Misalo tried to sound confident.

"Wait, can Carlo even fight?" I asked.

"Oh, yeah. From what I've heard, Carlo has a reputation. Several people have told me that Carlo has gotten into fights where he's knocked guys out."

"Doesn't that scare you?" I asked.

"I don't know. Should it?" he asked.

"Okay, so you're not afraid at all?" I asked.

"I don't have time to be afraid. I hate the guy's guts," he said with absolute conviction.

"Why? Because of Maya?" I had asked a question I really didn't want to know the answer to.

"It's about respect, Viviana. He disrespected me. You understand, don't you?" he asked.

I looked into his pretty eyes and reluctantly said, "Of course, baby. You know I understand."

Fourteen

MAYA

Normally I would have dreaded spending the day with my mom and sister, but my mother had been allowing me to drive just a little on the local residential streets, where I couldn't cause a traffic accident or run into anything. Last year my dad allowed me to get some practice driving at the cemetery. He told me I couldn't kill anyone there. For the first time in my life, I couldn't wait for school to start, just so I could go through driver's education. Once I had my driver's permit, it wouldn't be long before I got my driver's license. Then I wouldn't have to take the bus or walk everywhere anymore. I'd ask for the keys to the car and spend the day doing only the things I wanted to do.

Anna and I helped my mom unload our purchases from the trunk of her car and take them in the house. We'd purchased new pillows, bedspreads and a number of other household items that my mom insisted we needed. I had to give my mother credit. She knew how to budget well and keep the house running smoothly. For example, we never ran out of anything. I'd never experienced going to the bathroom, only to discover all the toilet paper had been used up. Keysha told me that happened all the time when she lived with her real mom.

"Girl, sometimes my mother wouldn't buy toothpaste, and I'd have to brush my teeth with baking soda," Keysha mentioned once.

"Eww. Gross," I said, frowning at the thought of putting baking soda in my mouth. "What did that taste like?"

"It was very grainy, like wet sand," Keysha said, cringing at the memory.

My mother was a very organized woman. She didn't like clutter, and an untidy house drove her insane. She'd taught Anna, Paul and me that it didn't take long to clean up. If we got into the habit of doing the dishes after dinner, then we wouldn't have to deal with them later. Another thing she insisted on was that we folded all laundry as soon as it was done. There was no leaving clothes in the dryer or a laundry hamper. All clothes had to be hung up or neatly folded in drawers.

"Maya, take these bedsheets upstairs and leave them for Viviana." My mother handed me a bag. When I didn't take the bag right away, she raised her voice at me. "I know you heard what I just said." She didn't know Viviana and I had gotten into a fight and weren't getting along. I unenthusiastically took the bag.

"Go on. Take it upstairs to her," she said as she began emptying another bag.

I walked upstairs and stood in the hallway at the top of the landing. The door to the room she shared with Anna was closed.

"Viviana." I called her name twice, but she didn't respond. I walked over to the door and pushed it open. Viviana was resting on her stomach, talking on the phone. "You could've at least answered me," I said with an unpleasant tone of voice.

Viviana looked at me as if I were totally meaningless to her. I sat the bag down and was about to walk out of the room when something stopped me. I looked closer at the jeans she was wearing. I'd never seen her wear those jeans and that top before. *I know doggone well she hasn't raided my closet,* I thought to myself as I turned and marched down the hall toward my bedroom. As I moved toward my closet, I noticed clothing tags sitting on my dresser.

"Oh, hell no!" I shouted as I ran back across the hallway. "Viviana!" I yelled at her.

She was engrossed in conversation and acted as if she was annoyed by the interruption.

"Why are you wearing my clothes?" I snarled at her.

"Listen, boo, I'm going to call you back. I've got to deal with something," Viviana said before ending her phone call. "What's your problem?" Vivian asked as she sat upright.

"What's my problem?" I snapped. "The problem is you're wearing my clothes!"

Viviana tugged at the top as if it were an old garment not worthy of me getting upset over. "You can stop yelling at me." Viviana's arrogance incensed me.

"Why did you go into my room and steal my clothes?" I waited for an explanation as I planned in my mind how I was going to attack her.

"First of all, I didn't *steal* anything," Viviana defiantly answered.

"Yes, you did. You went into my closet and stole my clothes!" I yelled.

"I didn't steal anything. If I were going to steal something, I wouldn't have brought it back. Besides, the tags were still on these clothes. It's not like you wore them already. You have so many clothes that you probably forgot you had this outfit." Viviana didn't seem to understand that what she'd done was very foul.

"Take my clothes off!" I said, moving closer to her. Win or lose, I was ready to fight her again, and I didn't care who knew about it.

"You want me to just take them off in front of you?" Viviana asked, as if she were now insulted.

"I'm not going to ask you again. Either you take off my things now or I'm going to put your head through a wall," I said, feeling my blood turn cold as ice.

"Fine. I planned on having the stuff cleaned first, but since you insist, I'll take them off now," Viviana said as she began to undress. She handed me my top and jeans. I held my clothing in one hand and shoved her back with the other.

"Stay out of my things," I snarled, fully expecting her to retaliate. Instead, a villainous smile spread across her face.

"I've taken more than clothes away from you, honey." Viviana laughed.

"What are you talking about?" I asked, only half interested in what she was saying.

"You'll find out sooner or later." Viviana opened a dresser drawer and pulled out a pair of shorts and a T-shirt.

"Hey, what's going on?" Anna asked as she walked into the room.

I glanced at Viviana with disgust. "Nothing," I said as I walked out. I went into my room and checked around to make sure Viviana hadn't taken anything else. Then I got a brilliant idea. I went back downstairs and searched around the house for my dad. I found him in the garage, where he was changing the oil on his car.

"Daddy," I said to him sweetly.

"Yeah, ladybug?" he said, calling me by his nickname for me.

"I want to get a lock for my bedroom," I whined, hoping to get him to agree without having him ask why. Instead I got the opposite reaction.

"Why?" he asked.

"Because there are people in this house who don't respect privacy or the property of others," I complained.

"Has your brother been pestering you again?" My father was totally clueless.

"Dad, can you please just put a lock on my bedroom door?" I pleaded with him.

"No. I don't like the idea of locks on bedroom doors, especially the bedroom door of a teenager," he said, grabbing a nearby rag to wipe motor oil from his fingers.

"Dad, it's Viviana. She's a total nuisance. Trust me, please." I tried to give him my best sad-faced ladybug look, but now that I was seventeen, it didn't have the same impact that it had when I was seven.

"Ladybug, I know that having your cousin, Viviana, stay with us isn't easy. You have to be a little compassionate and understanding. She's been through a tough time, and she isn't as blessed as you are."

"Are you serious?" I couldn't believe he'd allow Viviana to blind him with her bull.

"Yes. She's going to be with us for a while. We all have to make adjustments and a little more room in our hearts." He tried to reason with me, but I didn't want to hear another word that fell out of his mouth.

I crossed my arms and pouted.

"Do you want me or your mother to make a general announcement that everyone needs to be respectful of your space and belongings?" he asked.

"Just forget it, Dad. I see that you have a new ladybug in your life," I grumbled as I turned and walked back inside the house.

The following day, after I finished with my chores, my plan was to go over to Keysha's house and hang out with her, but she was hanging out with her grandmother Katie, who'd come to town for a visit. Since I really didn't feel like hanging around the house, I checked online for the start times of movies and then decided to catch the bus to the movie theater. When I got there, I paid for my ticket and walked inside. The popcorn smelled extra good, so I decided to stand in the long concession line. Just as I placed my order for a combination popcorn and soda, some guy walked up and said, "Can I pay for your snack?" Startled, I turned to see Carlo standing next to me.

"What are you doing here?" I asked.

"Last time I checked, this was a free country," he said.

"Stop being a smart-ass," I said.

"Okay. Would you like it better if I was a dumb ass?" He laughed.

"No," I said, suddenly feeling nervous.

"You don't mind, do you?" He reached for his wallet as the cashier placed my food on the counter.

"Will that be all?" asked the cashier.

"No. I'll take a large combo," Carlo said.

"Why are you paying for my food, and why do I keep running into you?" I asked.

"Well, why not pay for your food?" he said, answering my question with one of his own. "As far as your ability to be at all the places I am, I'd have to say you're following me. What movie are you here to see?"

"This one." I showed him my ticket stub.

"Oh, this is just too funny." He pulled out his ticket stub and showed it to me. We'd both paid to see the same film.

"I think you're the one who is following me." I was suddenly suspicious. "Are you here with your girlfriend or something?" I asked.

"Well, if I had a girlfriend, you'd be the first to know about her." Carlo looked at me with his dreamy eyes. I had to force myself not to fall for any tricks he might be trying to play.

"So, you just happened to come to the movie theater today by yourself?" I asked, for clarification.

"Yes. Is there a crime against that?" he asked.

"No," I answered.

"And you? Are you here with that bonehead, Misalo?" he asked.

I didn't like the fact that he'd called Misalo a bonehead, but I didn't say anything. I didn't see any point in it. "No. I'm here alone, as well."

"Wow. It's as if fate is saying we should be together," Carlo said as he paid for our snacks.

I took my food and moved over to the station where the napkins and straws were.

"So, why don't we sit together in the movie?" Carlo suggested.

"I don't care," I answered, wondering if I'd inadvertently just agreed to a date.

Carlo and I walked into the dark movie theater and took two middle seats just below the window of the projection booth. Just as we got situated, the movie previews began and the theater got even darker. During the movie, Carlo positioned his leg so that it was touching mine. I sat for a few minutes, wondering if it would be rude of me to reposition my body so that there was no contact. I couldn't believe I was having that type of mental debate with myself, but I was. I finally decided that there was no harm being done.

As the movie progressed, Carlo decided to be a little bolder by placing his hand on my knee. "This is a great movie. I'm so glad we're seeing it together," whispered Carlo, leaning close to me.

I was confused. I didn't know if I should just go with the flow and allow Carlo to continue touching me or if I should spoil everything and hurt his feelings by asking him to remove his hand. Then, out of the clear blue, the scent of his cologne wafted through the air and excited my sense of smell. I wanted to be sure the sweet scent was on his body, so I leaned closer to him. I craned my nose upward, toward his earlobe, and sure enough, Carlo smelled good. I guess he took my leaning closer as a hint to put his arm around me. I immediately froze up.

"Are you cold? I could run to my car and grab a jacket for you," he offered.

"No," I whispered softly. "I'm okay."

"Good." Carlo held on to me for the remainder of the movie. Although I felt uneasy at first, after I relaxed, I realized that being in his arms didn't feel as horrible as I'd imagined. When the movie ended, we walked out into the hallway.

"I have to go to the bathroom," I said to him. Before he could respond, I walked away. When I came out, Carlo was waiting for me.

"You didn't have to wait," I said, feeling bad.

"Well, I thought it would be rude of me to just leave without at least saying goodbye," Carlo pointed out as we made our way toward the exit doors.

"I wouldn't have held it against you," I assured him.

"You say that now, but you know that if you had come out of the restroom and hadn't seen me, you would have been disappointed." Carlo chuckled.

"No, I would have been cool—"

"Shhh," Carlo said with his index finger on his lips. "Would you like to hang out with me this afternoon?"

"Uh…"

"If you have something to do, I totally understand," he said quickly, offering me a way out.

"No, it's not that," I sighed.

"Then what is it?" he asked.

"What did you have in mind?" I said, giving in. I

knew that my relationship with Misalo was on the brink of crumbling apart forever. And if I was truly going to get over him, I needed to date other guys.

"I want to take you someplace special," Carlo said.

"I hope you don't think you're going to take me someplace so that you can try to get some booty," I replied, quickly letting him know I wasn't the type of girl who was going to do anything just because he was handsome.

"No." Carlo smiled. "The place I want to take you is outdoors."

"Okay," I agreed. Carlo held out his hand for me to place mine in. I stared at his palm for a moment before finally giving him my hand. Together we walked out of the theater and stepped out into the warm sunlight. I reached into my purse and removed a pair of sunglasses.

"You look like a Hollywood movie star with those glasses." Carlo smiled at me.

"What? You didn't know that I was famous? I'm practically related to Selma Hayek," I said jokingly.

"One thing is for sure. You're better looking than she is," Carlo replied, complimenting me. I knew he was only trying to win points, but I had to admit, he was doing pretty well with his last comment.

I had no idea where Carlo was taking me, and for some strange reason I didn't care. I was actually very happy to be getting away, if only for a few hours. We climbed in Carlo's car, Carlo hopped on the highway and we drove to the small town of Monee, Illinois. We drove down some back roads until we reached the Monee Reservoir, which was where Carlo parked. I stepped out and took in my surroundings. I'd never been there before. It was a very peaceful place. There was plenty of open prairie as far as my eyes could see and a beautiful lake, where people were out enjoying a lazy afternoon, floating around in paddleboats.

"How did you ever find this place?" I asked, noticing a nearby concession stand that sold refreshments and fishing gear.

"When I was young, my uncle used to bring me here to go fishing. Just beyond those trees over there is where the fishing is pretty good." Carlo pointed to the area he was speaking fondly of.

"I've never been fishing in my life," I said, and the image of placing a worm on a hook made my skin crawl.

"You should try it. It's lots of fun," Carlo replied.

"Oh, no, you've got the wrong girl if you're looking for someone to go fishing with," I said as I walked toward the pier.

"I'm going to go rent a paddleboat," Carlo uttered as he headed toward a nearby rental stand.

When I got to the pier, I placed my hand on the wooden rail just as a warm summer breeze caressed my skin.

"It's peaceful, isn't it?" Carlo approached me from behind and pressed his chest against my back. I should've stepped away, but I didn't. Carlo pulled my hair away from my neck and boldly placed sweet kisses on my neck, near the back of my ear. My body tingled at his touch. It was all too easy to get caught up in the rapture of the moment.

"You should give me a chance, Maya. I'd never hurt you or mistreat you," Carlo said earnestly.

"I know. I don't think you would, at least not on purpose," I admitted, trying my best not to completely surrender to him.

Carlo moved to the other side of my neck and kissed me more. He then gently tugged on my shoulder so that I'd turn around and face him. He placed his index finger under my chin and lifted it up. He gazed into my eyes, caressed my cheek and said, "You have very soft skin."

"Thank you," I answered as he leaned in to kiss me. I closed my eyes, and the moment my lips met his, I felt a tingling sensation rush through my body. "Wow! We'd better slow down," I said, placing the palm of my hand on his chest.

"Sure. Come on. Let's go out on the water." Carlo took my hand and led me down to the dock where the paddleboats were. Carlo and I got on, positioned ourselves, and with a little skillful maneuvering, we guided the boat toward the horizon.

"Can I ask you a personal question?" Carlo asked.

"Sure," I said, not giving his question much thought.

"The photos you took for Misalo… Why did he disrespect you and forward them to so many people? I'm sure by now you know they've gone viral."

"Why did you bring that up? Have you seen them, too?" I was embarrassed and lowered my head to mask my humiliation.

Somberly, Carlo said, "Yes. I saw them. I thought they were hot, along with every guy in the neighborhood, I'm sure." Carlo reached over and held my hand. "It's okay. If anyone ever gives you a hard time or teases you about it, you let me know and I'll deal with them."

"How, Carlo? There is nothing that can be done at this point." I sighed, wishing I'd never taken the photos.

"I'll make them shut up and leave you alone." Carlo cracked his knuckles. "If they don't, I'll make them. Just like I'm going to make Misalo sorry that he ever disrespected you and me."

Rubbing my temples in an effort to prevent a migraine headache from forming, I asked, "What are you talking about, Carlo?"

"When I see that chump again, I'm going to beat him down." Carlo's words horrified me.

"But why?" I asked, completely dismayed as I looked up at him.

"Well, for starters we have a score to settle. Because of him, I lost my job. You saw how he started the fight that day at the mall. Then I want to beat him down for ruining your reputation. I hear guys talking all the time about how they'd love to do stuff with you and to you. They think you're a slutty girl, but I know that's not true." Carlo wanted to display nobility and defend my honor, name and reputation. I admired him for wanting to be my hero, but I didn't want him to hurt Misalo.

"Can't you just let all of that go?" I asked, hoping he could find it in his heart to move on.

"No, Maya. Misalo has gone too far and he's going to pay, one way or another." I noticed that Carlo's eyes were ablaze with contempt and hatred for Misalo.

I suddenly didn't want to be out on the lake with Carlo. All I wanted was to go back home, call Keysha and figure out what I should do.

Fifteen

VIVIANA

NOW that Misalo and I were an item, I desperately wanted to look prettier and be better than Maya. If the idea of comparing the two of us ever crossed Misalo's mind in any way, I wanted to make sure I was clearly the better choice. I wanted my hair to look better, my skin to feel softer and my body to be shapelier. I never wanted him to second-guess anything when thoughts of me ran across his mind. Whenever he daydreamed about me, I wanted him to be able to remember the scent of my skin and the silky feel of my hair against his cheeks. I wanted Misalo to be totally into me, and I planned to do whatever it took to make sure he never wanted to be with another girl.

I would always keep it real with Misalo and never act like a helpless princess who needed to be rescued. I would be the type of girl who knew how to be a lady but could flip the script by pulling off my shoes, tying up my hair and throwing down if the situation called for it.

In order to make my dream a reality, I needed money so that I could buy clothes, accessories and whatever else I would need to keep Misalo's attention focused on me.

Since I didn't have a job and was too embarrassed to just flat out ask my aunt Raven to overhaul my wardrobe, not that she wouldn't, I just preferred to do things on my own. The only option I was left with was to use my pickpocketing skills to get money and credit cards to finance my endeavor.

I tried to remember everything that I'd learned from Toya Taylor, a girl who was once my friend and who'd taught me a lot about pickpocketing. I gathered a few things I'd need to help me conceal the items that I'd end up taking from unsuspecting strangers and headed for the front door. My plan was to hang out at the mall, find some easy targets, make my move and max out any live credit card that fell into my possession. Just as I was about to walk out of the house, my uncle Herman caught me.

"Hey, Viviana," he said, walking toward me, carrying a laundry basket filled with clothes.

"Hey," I answered back, not wanting to get into a long conversation with him.

"Do you want to tell me where you're headed?" he asked.

I wanted to say, "What are you, a freaking detective now?" but I knew a response like that would land me in hot water.

I gave him a vague answer. "Just out."

He questioned me like he'd never done before. "What do you mean just out? Out where?" He set the basket of laundry down, stood with his feet shoulder width apart and folded his arms across his chest. Uncle Herman was wearing blue jeans and a black tank top. Although his stomach looked rather bloated today, his arms were muscular and strong. He didn't look like he was in the mood for playing any games.

"To the store," I answered slowly, trying not to sound condescending.

"What store?" he asked.

At that moment, I knew I had to do something to soften him up. "Are you worried about me?" I asked, walking back toward him.

"I just don't like the idea of you coming and going anytime you see fit without letting anyone know where you are," he said as I stood directly in front of him and looked up into his eyes. I blinked my eyes a few times and tried my best to look totally innocent. I used to do that sort of thing with my dad, and it worked like a charm.

"I'm sorry. I didn't mean to upset you by not saying where I'd be. In the future I'll make sure that someone knows where I am. Besides, you can always call me on my cell phone," I reminded him.

"I know that, Viviana. This is about respect for the house and family," he explained.

"Do you think I'm being disrespectful?" I asked innocently.

"Yes, a little," he said.

"I'm so sorry, Uncle Herman," I said and gave him a big hug, making sure to smash my cheek into his chest. "I don't mean to be a burden on you."

Placing his hands on my shoulders, Uncle Herman gently pushed me away so that he could look into my eyes. "You're welcome to stay here for as long as necessary, Viviana, but there are going to be rules that you must follow."

"Okay," I answered pleasantly. When he smiled down at me, I knew that I'd won him over.

I came up with a really good lie that I knew he wouldn't challenge. "I'm going to the corner pharmacy to pick up some personal items. Is that okay?" I asked. Uncle Herman's jaw dropped a little, and I could tell that he immediately understood that I was trying to tell him I was running out only to pick up hygiene products.

"Oh, sure." He paused. "Do you need your aunt Raven to go with you? She can drive you."

"No. I'm a big girl. I can handle this one on my own," I said, smiling at him.

"Do you need money?" he asked, reaching for his wallet. I wasn't about to stop him from giving me cash.

"Sure," I said.

"How much do you need?" he asked as I peeked into his wallet. I saw a fifty-dollar bill and what appeared to be several twenty-dollar bills.

"Fifty dollars should cover what I need," I said, waiting for him to give it to me.

"I'll make sure that your aunt makes a mental note to keep up with all the things you girls need," Uncle Herman said.

I leaned close to him and whispered, "I'll make sure she knows so that you don't have to feel embarrassed."

"Oh, I'm not embarrassed if you're not," he said.

Not wanting my lie to go any further than it already had, I said, "Okay, are we done here?"

"Yes," he answered.

"Okay. I'll be back in a little while," I said.

"Are you sure you don't want Anna or Maya to go with you?" he asked as I opened the front door.

"Yes, I am positive," I said as I walked out.

When I arrived at the River Oaks Center, I hung out at the food court, which was overflowing with shoppers taking time to grab a quick bite to eat. According to Toya Taylor, I was to keep an eye out for easy targets. As luck would have it, I spotted the perfect victim. A woman had just paid for her food with a credit card, and instead of placing the card back inside her purse, she had placed it in the side pocket of the suit jacket she was wearing. I immediately placed myself on a collision course with her. My plan was to bump into her "accidentally," reach into her pocket, lift the credit card and discreetly walk away.

I took one last deep breath before I moved in to execute my plan.

"Oh, I'm so sorry," I said the moment I bumped into the lady. I touched her shoulder with my left hand so that all of her attention was focused away from my right hand, which had successfully slipped into her pocket and retrieved the credit card.

I continued talking to the stranger. "I'm so clumsy. I wasn't paying attention. Are you okay?" Judging solely by the clothes she was wearing, I assumed she was a businesswoman who'd decided to grab something to eat at the mall's food court.

"It's okay," she said, assuring me that no harm had been done.

I smiled at her and apologized once more before casually moving on. I made a loop around the food court and left the area as quickly as I could, before the woman discovered her credit card was missing. The first store I hit was Wet Seal. I hastily found a rack of blue jeans that were my size. A salesgirl, who was not much older than I was, walked over to me and asked if I needed help. I decided to make small talk with her. I figured that if I befriended her, she'd be more than happy to ring up the sale without asking for identification.

I asked a silly question. "Do you have these jeans in pink?"

The salesgirl tucked her sandy-brown hair behind her ear and smiled. "I wish," she said.

"I think these jeans would look so hot in pink," I continued, which only encouraged the salesgirl to keep talking.

Looking around the rack, the salesgirl found a similar pair of jeans in red. "What do you think about these?" she asked.

"Oh, those are nice," I said, reaching out and touching the fabric.

"Would you like to try them on?" she asked with a cheerful smile.

In the back of my mind, I was telling myself not to waste too much time. If the businesswoman realized she'd lost her credit card, it would take her only a minute or two to contact her credit card company and report it lost.

"No. I know these are my size. They should fit perfectly," I said, attempting to sound as gleeful as the salesgirl.

"Are you sure? Sometimes jeans can fit a little funny," she said, crinkling her nose.

"I'm sure. The brand fits me well. What do you think about this brown pair?" I asked, holding them up for her to see.

"Chocolate jeans are so cool," she said. She turned around, as if she were searching for something. "I believe those have a top that goes with them." She stepped away for a brief moment.

I nervously raced through the rack of jeans and found two more pairs in my size. When the salesgirl returned, she'd located the perfect top.

"Oh, that is hot," I said, giving the salesgirl her kudos.

"There are some more tops over there, if you'd like to take a look," she suggested.

"You know, I'm sort of on a budget. I'll take the jeans that I have and the top you brought over."

"Okay. Follow me and I'll ring everything up for you," she said cheerfully. I followed her to the counter, where she rang everything up before folding the merchandise and placing it in a shopping bag. "Okay. Your total is $145.37."

I pulled out the fifty-dollar bill Uncle Herman had given me, making sure the salesgirl saw it. I then briefly searched my small purse, as if I was looking for more money. I huffed a little, as if I was annoyed, before handing her the stolen credit card. Without hesitating, the girl swiped the card and waited. When I heard the sound of the receipt printing, I exhaled. She handed the credit card back to me, and for the first time, I read the name on it.

It belonged to Barbara Kendall. I paused in thought for a moment, trying to remember where I'd heard that last name before. Then I realized that the last name of Maya's best friend, Keysha, was Kendall. I told myself that there was no way they could be related, because Keysha didn't look anything like the lady I'd stolen the credit card from. Anyway, I quietly thanked Barbara Kendall for not realizing her credit card had been stolen.

"Here you go. Have a great day," said the salesgirl.

"You, too," I said as I rushed out of the store.

Next, I hit 5.7.9, then Body Central, Lady Foot Locker and The Limited. I was having a ball with the stolen credit card. I spent nearly a thousand dollars and would have kept going, but I had too many bags. I had shoes, jeans, tops, accessories, a decent dress and even something to work out in with Misalo from J. C. Penney. I was on a high. I wanted to stash the stuff I'd already gotten and go back and keep charging until the card was declined, but I couldn't. I had to take what I had and head home.

I decided to break the fifty-dollar bill by buying a snack so that I'd have change to catch the bus back to the house. During the short ride home, I thought about Toya Taylor and was thankful for what she'd taught me. I now fully understood why she took so many risks. It was because the reward was so great.

When I returned home, I entered the house through the basement door so that no one would see all the shopping bags and start asking questions I didn't want to answer. The laundry basket Uncle Herman was using earlier was sitting in front of the dryer.

"Perfect," I said aloud as I opened the lid and placed all my purchases inside the basket. I broke down the shoe boxes and placed them inside the shopping bags. I then took all the evidence outside and placed it inside the neighbor's trash can. I went back inside the house, snatched up the laundry basket and went upstairs to try on all my purchases.

I was standing in front of the bedroom mirror, pivoting in all directions to make sure that the outfit I had on made my butt look big but not sloppy, and that my tummy didn't look poky. I had to admit that, even though I had been totally nervous and had grabbed items in a rush, I didn't do too badly as far as coordinating outfits went. What I currently had on—a gorgeous soft blue top with chocolate jeans that accented my every curve, a thick braided jean belt and a pair of fold-over scrunch boots—was a perfect ensemble.

"Where did you get those clothes?" Maya asked, startling me. She was standing in the doorway, looking bewildered. She gave me the same look the evil stepsisters gave Cinderella when they saw how fabulous she looked in her blue evening gown.

"None ya'," I said sarcastically.

"None ya?" Maya repeated. I'd clearly confused the hell out of her.

"Yeah, none of your business. Get it?" I said and was about to slam the door in her face, but she stepped inside.

"I swear, if you've been in my closet again, I'll pour hot grease on you while you're sleeping," Maya said, attempting to strike fear in my heart.

"First of all, you and I don't even have the same style," I retorted, raising my voice at her.

"You could've fooled me! Last time I checked, you

were taking stuff out of my private collection. Just admit it, Viviana. You want to be like me so bad, but you can't."

"I'd rather have God turn me into a pimple on a frog's butt before I'd ever want to be like you," I said unapologetically.

"Be careful what you wish for," Maya warned me.

"Why are you up here bothering me?" I threaded my eyebrows together. "Don't you have better things to do than spy on me?"

"Someone has to keep an eye on you," Maya said with attitude.

"Whatever, trick!" I said, turning my focus back to my reflection in the mirror.

"You'd better watch who you're calling a trick, slut," Maya answered back, wanting to have a battle of wits with me.

I turned, faced her and pointed my finger at her. "Word on the street is that you've taken top slut honors for the year with those photos you took," I said, wanting to make sure my words bit her. The expression that formed on Maya's face was priceless. "Yeah, I saw them, too." I mimicked the way she'd posed in one of her photos, and then laughed. I could see tears forming in her eyes.

"I came up here to tell you that dinner is ready," she informed me before rushing away.

"Whatever," I muttered as I headed to the bathroom to wash my hands for dinner.

I called Misalo as soon as I got up the next morning, but he didn't answer his phone. I called him again an hour later and once again got no answer. I called him a third and fourth time, and still my calls went unanswered. At that point, I sent him a text message and asked him why he was ignoring me. It took fifteen minutes for him to respond with a text message.

Misalo: Huh?

Viviana: Y r u not answering my calls?

Misalo: R u trying to stalk me now?

Viviana: Do u think I am?

Misalo: A little.

Viviana: Fine. I will never call again.

Misalo: No need 2 get mad.

Viviana: I don't like to be blown off.

Misalo: Who said I was blowing u off?

Viviana: Feels like u r.

Misalo: I've been with my dad all morning and still with him. We r driving.

Viviana: O. Sorry.

Misalo: U just assume things.

Viviana: I know. My bad.

Misalo: So u were thinking about me?

Viviana: Duh, of course I was.

Misalo: What were u thinking?

Viviana: Do u really want to know?

Misalo: Yes.

Viviana: I'm hot and need u to cool me off.

Misalo: O snap. LOL.

Viviana: What does that mean?

Misalo: Means that I want more details.

Viviana: Do I have to spell it out 4 u?

Misalo: Yup.

Viviana: When is ur birthday?

Misalo: It has already passed. It was June 3.

Viviana: Well. Mine is coming up and I want birthday sex.

Misalo: 4 real?

Viviana: U got a problem with that?

Misalo: No. When and where?

Viviana: LOL. Now u want to see me real bad don't u?

Misalo: Yes.

Viviana: How bad?

Misalo: Real bad. So when do u wanna hook up?

Viviana: Did u ever have sex with Maya?

Misalo: Y u asking that?

Viviana: Because I want to know.

Misalo: We've done some things.

Viviana: That wasn't a real answer.

Misalo: Yes it was.

Viviana: Did u go all the way with her?

Misalo: Does it matter?

Viviana: R u still a virgin?

Misalo: R u?

Viviana: What do u think?

Misalo: I think ur just teasing me.

Viviana: So now u think I'm just being a tease?

Misalo: Yes.

Viviana: Well I guess I'll just have to prove u wrong.

Misalo: Please do. U know how much I like a girl who can prove herself. R u that girl?

Viviana: I am trying to be.

Misalo: Good. U think u can get free tonight?

Viviana: Y? U trying to make me prove it tonight?

Misalo: Thought u would like to go roller-skating but if u want me to cool u off then I'm game.

Viviana: I would love to go roller-skating.

Misalo: What about hooking up for other stuff?

Viviana: I'll plan it and let u know. What time u wanna pick me up?

Misalo: U know I can't come to the house right?

Viviana: Oh yeah. I forgot. U can pick me up at the corner.

Misalo: Cool. I'll see u around 6:00.

Viviana: Okay. I plan on looking extra sexy 4 u.

Misalo: I would like that.

Viviana: TTYL.

Once I was done making plans with Misalo, an awesome idea came to mind. I thought I would be able to prove my loyalty to him even more if I started buying him clothes. That way, whenever he wore an item, he'd think about me all day. He'd be wearing fashions by Viviana. The silly thought caused me to laugh aloud, but the more I thought about it, the more sense it made. I quickly checked the clock to see if I had enough time to rush to the mall and find him something. I had just enough time to rush out, buy something and get back before 6:00 p.m. Without giving the idea any more thought, I got myself together, took Barbara Kendall's credit card and headed out the door.

When I arrived at the mall, I went into Sears and located a nice blue-and-white-striped polo shirt for Misalo. I went to the counter, crossed my fingers and prayed the credit card would go through.

"I'm sorry, Ms. Kendall, but this card has been declined," said the male sales rep. "Do you have another form of payment?"

In order to avoid total embarrassment, I paid with the remainder of the fifty bucks Uncle Herman had given to me the day before.

Like clockwork, Misalo was at the corner to pick me up at exactly the time he said he would. I got in the car, got situated and removed the purchase from the bag.

"Look at what I brought you today, boo," I said, holding up the polo shirt.

Misalo glanced over at it and smiled. "That's nice. Thank you. You didn't have to get me anything," he said as he flicked the turn signal before making a right turn.

"Consider it a belated birthday gift. I'm so glad you like it," I said as I stuffed it back inside the bag. I knew he'd try it on for me later.

We arrived at the Lynwood roller-staking rink about ten minutes later. When we went inside, loud music was playing and there were plenty of people there having fun. Misalo and I walked over to the shoe counter, where he paid for our roller skates. We found a place to sit and change our shoes.

"So, when are you going to find more time to show me how to throw those combination punches?" Misalo asked.

"Whenever you want me to, baby," I said, willing to do whatever he commanded me to.

"How about tomorrow? We could meet at my friend Matt's house. He has a punching bag set up in his basement."

"Okay. What time do you want me to be there?" I asked.

"Well, his parents leave for work around eight in the morning, so to be on the safe side, let's say at nine-thirty. I'll give you a call and tell you where he lives."

"Is it really far?" I asked.

"No. You can walk to his house from where you live, or I could come pick you up," Misalo assured me.

"Whatever. We'll work it out," I said as I slipped my foot into a roller skate. Once I had both feet in, I carefully stood up but immediately lost my balance and fell back down onto the seat. "Oh, this is not going to be as easy as I thought," I said as I attempted to stand once again.

"When was the last time you went roller-skating?" Misalo asked.

"Honestly?" I asked, looking at him.

"Yes," he said as he tied up the laces on his roller skates and then stood up.

"When I was a little girl, I had pink roller skates that I used to roll down the sidewalk on near my grandmother's house."

"Oh, so it has been a very long time." Misalo chuckled.

"I'm just a little rusty, that's all. I promise not to embarrass you," I said, rising to my feet once again.

"Come on." Misalo reached for my hand and guided me toward the rink. I wobbled a lot as we moved closer to an area where we could join in on the fun.

"You go ahead," I insisted, fearing that I'd only make us both look like fools if I fell flat on my behind.

"Come on. I'll make sure you don't fall," Misalo said, trying to make me feel comfortable.

"No, seriously. You go on. When I'm ready, I'll come on out there." I tried to wave him on, but he wouldn't go.

"Tell you what. Why don't we go over there to the small practice rink? There are hardly any people over there. You could roll around until you get the swing of it." Misalo pointed to the rink he was suggesting we head to.

"Okay. That sounds like a good plan," I said as I clumsily wheeled myself in the direction of the smaller rink.

Misalo was very patient with me, even though I fell on my behind so many times I lost count. He never once complained, and I adored him for it.

sixteen

MAYA

I was sitting in my room, at my computer, surfing the internet for articles that even remotely talked about the drama I was going through. I had visited several sites that had blog posts about relationship dilemmas, such as what to do if your boyfriend was cheating on you or how to help him with personal grooming. I was hopelessly searching when I stumbled across an article that asked the question, "Is it bad to flirt with other guys if you have a boyfriend?" I read the answer, which said it was okay as long as no lines were crossed. The article went on to say that it was natural for a girl to want the attention of other guys. I thought about that statement for a moment. I wondered if I was subconsciously seeking out the attention of other guys out of some hidden insecurity. Maybe when I met Carlo, I sort of just wanted to see if I could get his attention. The more questions I asked myself, the more confused I became. I was about to continue surfing when I received a notification of an incoming video call on my computer. I read the notification and saw that it was Keysha, finally getting back to me. I clicked the button to accept the call and waited for her image to appear.

"Well, it's about time you got back to me," I said, noticing Keysha adjusting her webcam.

"I'm sorry. It has been sort of crazy around here," Keysha said, focusing her attention on me. "What are you wearing?" she asked.

"A T-shirt and sweatpants. Why? Do I look bad or something?" I asked, tugging at my pink T-shirt.

"No, you look fine. I was just being nosy," Keysha said as she leaned back in her seat. She had a funny look on her face. Judging by her look, I knew something was off.

"Keysha, are you okay?" I asked.

"Yeah, I'm also trying to listen to Barbara yell at my brother, Mike. She's been in a really crabby mood ever since her credit card was stolen," Keysha said.

"Her credit card was stolen?" I wasn't sure if I'd heard her right.

"Yeah, and the person who stole it went on a one-thousand-dollar shopping spree," Keysha said, then enlightened me on the seriousness of the situation.

"Really. Does your stepmom know what they bought?" I asked, wanting to get more details from her.

"The credit card company told her the stores where the card had been used. Whoever stole it shopped at stores Barbara doesn't go to, like Wet Seal. Barbara has her suspicions that some teenager took her credit card," Keysha said as she rested her elbows on the desktop and threaded her fingers together before resting her chin on top of her knuckles.

"I could see that happening," I said, thinking about the amount of traffic that was at River Oaks Center at any given time.

"Barbara canceled the credit card and even called the credit bureaus and told them what happened. She's afraid that whoever did this may try to steal her identity." Keysha rubbed the tip of her nose before she sneezed.

"Bless you," I said.

"Thanks."

"Why would someone want to steal her identity?" I asked.

"To buy stuff they couldn't otherwise afford. My grandmother Rubylee is like that. I'm not sure if I ever told you, but when I first moved in with my dad, I wrote her a letter to see how she was doing. When she wrote me back, she asked me to snoop around the house and send her all of his personal information, like bank records."

"Dang! Your grandmother Rubylee is rough," I said and then paused. "Speaking of snooping around, do you know that I caught Viviana snooping around in my parents' bedroom?"

"Really? Why would she be in there?" Keysha asked.

"She claimed that she thought Anna was in there, but I knew she was lying. She's so sneaky," I said.

"About your cousin, there is something I need to tell you, but I'm not sure if I should." Keysha rubbed the tip of her nose again and sneezed twice.

"Jeez. Do you have allergies or something?" I asked.

"Yeah, I do. Sometimes I sneeze, like, five or six times in a row," she explained as she reached for a tissue. "Hang on a second," she said, moving out of camera range. I listened to her as she blew her nose.

When she reappeared, I asked, "So, what is it that you're afraid to tell me?"

"No, you should go first. I know that you wanted to talk to me about Carlo," Keysha said.

I sighed before I began explaining my dilemma. "Carlo plans on beating up Misalo."

"What? Are you serious?" Keysha adjusted her webcam.

"Carlo said that he couldn't let Misalo disrespect him and get away with it. He's also ticked off at Misalo because he caused him to lose his job when they got into a fight at the mall. Plus, he wants to teach him a lesson for forwarding the private photos."

"Wow." Keysha leaned back in her seat and bit down on the tip of her index finger.

"What should I do? I tried to get Carlo to just forget about it, but he will not. I don't want to see Misalo hurt," I explained.

"Well, you may change your mind after I tell you this," Keysha said.

"It can't be any worse than what I'm already going through," I assured her.

"Do you know where Viviana was yesterday?" Keysha asked. I could tell she was stalling.

"I don't keep up with her. She could drop off the face of this earth, for all I care," I said unapologetically.

"When I tell you this, promise you will not get mad at me, okay?" Keysha waited for me to give my word.

"Okay, I promise not to get angry. Now, just tell me what your big secret is." I exhaled, then waited for Keysha to spill the beans.

"Last night Mike and Sabrina went out roller-skating. They saw Misalo and Viviana together."

"What!" I shouted. "What were they doing?"

"According to Mike, they were all booed up," Keysha explained.

"Booed up how?" I asked, wanting to hear every detail. I had had my suspicions about Viviana going for Misalo, but I never thought she'd stoop low enough to date my ex-boyfriend.

Keysha hesitated one last time before saying, "He saw them making out."

"What a sleazy, low-down, backstabbing slut!" I blurted out with utter disgust.

"Viviana is truly a piece of work," Keysha said, agreeing with my opinion of my cousin.

"I feel like a fool," I admitted.

"Why? None of this is your fault," Keysha reminded me.

"I feel like a fool because I tried to talk Carlo out of beating Misalo up," I said.

"I know you don't want to hear this, but if Misalo did to me what he did to you, I'd pay someone to kick his butt. Has he come clean as to why he sent the photos to everyone?"

I felt my emotions stirring deep inside me. I tried to control them and force myself not to cry. My bottom lip quivered and my voice trembled when I said, "No. He acts as if he has no clue as to what I'm talking about. He was more interested in proving that I was sneaking around with Carlo."

"Don't cry, Maya," Keysha said, truly concerned about my feelings.

"I can't help it. I'm so heartbroken. Hang on. I'll be right back," I said, stepping away from my webcam. I walked down the hallway to the bathroom, where I dried my tears and blew my nose. When I returned, Keysha was waiting patiently for me.

"Do you want me to come over?" Keysha asked.

"No, you don't have to. I'm hurt and I'm mad," I said, biting my bottom lip.

"So, what are you going to do?" Keysha asked.

"I don't know. I don't think there is anything I can do," I said.

"Once people learn of the fight between Misalo and Carlo, I have a feeling that a ton of people are going to show up to see how it all goes down," Keysha said.

"Carlo hasn't said anything else to me about it. Maybe he has given it some thought and will not go through with it," I said.

"Do you honestly believe that?" Keysha asked.

"No."

"Are you going to go and watch what happens?" Keysha asked.

"I don't know," I answered truthfully.

"Well, if I hear anything else, I'll let you know," Keysha said.

"Thanks. You're such a good BFF," I said.

"The best in the world," Keysha answered back.

"Maya!"

I heard my mother call my name from the bottom of the staircase. "Yeah?" I answered.

"I made lunch. Come on down and eat with everyone," my mom said.

"Okay. I'll be there in a minute," I yelled and then focused my attention back on Keysha.

"You have to go?" Keysha asked.

"Yeah, I have to go and break bread with the enemy," I said, feeling vindictive venom flowing through me.

"Call me back when you're done eating. I have to tell you what Wesley did," Keysha said.

"Wesley?" I was surprised that she'd brought him up.

"Yeah. I want to get your opinion on it," Keysha explained.

"Okay," I answered. "I'll give you a buzz once I'm done."

"Cool. Talk to you later," Keysha said, holding up her hand and waving goodbye. I returned the gesture before ending our computer connection.

I went into the kitchen and became immediately irritated at the sight of Viviana. Not only because she was dating Misalo, but also because she was sitting in my seat. My mom sat on the right side of my dad, and I always sat on his left side. Viviana had parked her big bubble behind on his left side, and I had an issue with that.

"Excuse me," I said, walking over to her. Viviana looked over her shoulder at me as if she was confused as to why I was standing behind her. "You're in my seat."

"What? There is assigned seating for lunch?" Viviana laughed at me. I wanted to claw her eyes out.

"Maya, sit next to your brother. It won't kill you," said my mom as she placed a bowl of mustard potato salad on the table.

"This is my seat, though. I always sit here," I griped.

"Seriously, Maya?" Viviana asked condescendingly.

I bit down on my bottom lip and gave her a look of disgust. That was when I noticed the clothes she was wearing. She'd been at my house for a while, and I'd never seen her wear that particular top.

"Come on, Maya," said my brother, who pulled out the chair for me. I sat down and got situated.

"Viviana is pretty smart," my dad announced as my mother set his food in front of him.

"Oh, yeah?" my mom said as she moved over to the countertop near the stove to grab another plate.

"I'll help you, Aunt Raven," Viviana said, rising out of her seat. That was when I noticed the True Religion blue jeans she was wearing. It was another article of clothing that I'd never seen before. I knew for a fact that she couldn't fit in Anna's clothes, and the jeans did not belong to me.

"We were playing Trivial Pursuit, and she beat me hands down twice," said my dad.

"Is that so? No one ever beats you at that game, babe. You're the only person I know who walks around with tidbits of random information," said my mother. It was true. My father prided himself on knowing something about any particular subject. He said that knowing something about a variety of topics was useful when he was talking with clients.

"Yeah. I think Viviana is naturally gifted." When my father said that, my stomach turned.

"Thank you, Uncle Herman." Viviana soaked up his compliments like a vacuum sucking up dirt.

"So, Viviana, what's up with the new clothes?" I asked suspiciously so that everyone would pay attention to her outfit.

Viviana spun her neck around so quickly, I thought for

sure she'd snapped it off. She shot hot daggers at me with her eyes, and I knew immediately that she didn't want to discuss how she'd come by her new clothes.

"Yeah, Viviana. I noticed you had some new clothes, as well. When did you go shopping, and why didn't you take me?" asked Anna. I really didn't like my little sister all that much, but at that moment, I wanted to give her a big hug for helping me place Viviana in the hot seat.

"I did a little shopping for myself. Is there a law against that?" Viviana answered sarcastically.

"Depends on where you got the money and where you went shopping," I said. In the back of my mind I was accusing her of stealing the clothes. There was no way she could afford the expensive jeans she was wearing.

Although I couldn't prove it, I wanted there to be a certain amount of suspicion surrounding her purchases.

"I had money saved up. My mom gave me a little and…" Viviana's voice trailed off. I could tell by the way she kept shifting her eyes from left to right that she was quickly trying to think of a convincing lie. "Grandmother Esmeralda also gave me a little money."

I thought to myself, No, she didn't just lie about our grandmother. "Yeah, right," I said, badgering her.

"Well, it's true. I got everything on sale, and I'm a good shopper, as well," Viviana said. "Besides, Uncle Herman also gave me fifty dollars. Trust me, I know how to stretch a dollar."

"You gave her fifty bucks, Dad?" asked my brother. "What's up with that? You still owe me twenty-five bucks for cleaning out the shed."

"Did you finish the job?" my dad asked my brother.

"Yeah. I told you that I had two days ago," my brother reminded him.

Snapping his fingers, my dad said, "That's right. I do remember you telling me. There is money in my bedroom, on the dresser. After lunch you can get it."

"Is that why you were in my parents' bedroom the other day, Viviana? Were you looking for money?" I asked, unwilling to extinguish the spotlight of suspicion that I was casting on her.

"What were you doing in our bedroom, Viviana?" my mother asked.

Shrugging her shoulders, Viviana said, "I was searching for Anna. I thought I heard her in there. That's all. I hope that's okay."

Oh, spare me your cordialness, I said to myself as I felt my resentment for her coming to a boil.

My mother finally sat down and blessed our food before we began eating.

My father continued to praise Viviana. "Like I was saying, Viviana would probably make a good contestant on a game show."

"Do you really think so, Uncle Herman?" Viviana leaned into him and playfully jabbed him with her elbow. If I could've stabbed Viviana in the neck with my fork and gotten away with it, I would have. The way she was sucking up to my dad was sickening.

"Yes. I think you're a very smart girl," my dad said. I couldn't take it anymore. I had to shatter the good girl image Viviana had sold to my dad. I had to let him know Viviana had about as much sense as God gave a rock.

Summoning my courage, I said, "Viviana is dating

Misalo, the boy you forbid me to date." I lowered my eyelids to slits as I glared at Viviana. I wanted her to see the flames of rage burning in my eyes.

"What?" My dad began choking on his food. My mother immediately got up, walked over to him and began slapping his back. Once my dad recovered, I repeated myself.

"I said she's dating Misalo. You remember him, don't you? He's the boy who took me to a dogfight."

"Viviana, is this true?" asked my mom.

"It's nothing serious." Viviana tried to downplay her role in the matter.

"That's not what I heard. I was told by an eyewitness that you were totally making out with him and practically having sex with him in the parking lot of the roller-skating rink." I couldn't believe I'd said all of that. I had got caught up in my anger and wanted Viviana to feel the heat of my hatred.

My dad turned to Viviana and said, "I don't think it's a good idea to date him." I'd gotten the reaction out of him that I wanted.

"Why would you want to date Maya's ex-boyfriend? That's kind of tacky, don't you think?" my mom asked, jumping on my "I hate Viviana" bandwagon.

Viviana shrugged. "He's a very nice guy and a great kisser, too." I knew Viviana's comment was meant for me, but I didn't care at that point.

"Has your mom had a conversation with you about boys and sex and protection?" asked my mom.

Viviana looked at my mom as if she was horrified. Deep inside, I was laughing at her.

"Yes, Viviana, are you sexually active?" I blurted out. My little brother started giggling.

"That's none of your business!" Viviana snapped at me.

"But it is my business," my mother remarked.

"What are you talking about?" asked Viviana.

"I'm talking about sex." My mom was not at all embarrassed to talk about it.

"Okay, can we, like, have this conversation some other time?" Viviana was clearly uncomfortable, and I loved it.

My dad chimed in. "You need to be smarter when it comes to boys, Viviana. Misalo was the reason Maya ended up with a broken leg. Besides, it's not cool to date the ex of a family member. Your aunt Raven is right. That's just tacky on your part."

"Real tacky," I added.

"I like him. He didn't marry Maya. It's not like I stole her husband or something. He was fair game," Viviana replied, defending her relationship with Misalo.

"It's your safety we're concerned about Viviana," said my mom.

Viviana got defensive and raised her voice. "So, what are you saying? I can't date?"

"Of course you can date. You just can't date him," said my mom.

"How are you going to tell me who I can and can't date? You can't control who I choose to like," Viviana screeched at my mom. She was teetering on the edge of being disrespectful.

"Watch your tone of voice, Viviana," my dad warned her. I could see tears welling up in her eyes. I knew she was trying extra hard to win my dad over and disappointing him would hurt her deeply.

"Misalo is nothing like you're making him out to be. He's a very nice guy. Nicer than any other guy I've ever liked. He's thoughtful, sincere, and I'm not going to give him up," Viviana said defiantly.

"Oh, yes, you are," I blurted out. I didn't mean to say what I was thinking. I just couldn't stomach her talking about Misalo as if they were truly in love. That not only made my skin crawl, but it also deepened my disdain for her.

"Misalo isn't nearly as bad as the guy Maya's dating."

I looked over at my little sister, Anna, who'd decided to see her way into the conversation. "What are you talking about?" I asked, annoyed by her attempt to shift the focus to me.

"You're dating someone, Maya?" asked my mom. She waited for me to answer her. Both my mom and dad insisted on keeping track of every guy I was dating.

"Anna doesn't know what she's talking about." I desperately wanted to discredit Anna's words.

"Yes, I do know what I'm talking about. Maya is dating Carlo, the boy I used to like, until I ended up in the hospital after mistaking meth for candy when I was at his house."

Before I could stop myself, I hurled a string of curses at Anna.

seventeen

VIVIANA

"I hate Maya. I hate Maya. I hate Maya!" Anna muttered as she walked into her bedroom in tears. I was trailing behind her because Uncle Herman had come down on both her and Maya hard for arguing at the dinner table. He was not happy about the undeniable animosity between them.

"I hate her, too," I chimed in as Anna rested on her bed with her face buried in her pillow. I sat on the floor beside her bed. "Sometimes she can be so mean," I said, resting my head against the bed.

"I seriously think she has some kind of mental disorder and she needs professional help," Anna said tearfully.

"Anna, don't allow her to make you cry," I said, trying to cheer her up.

"Why does she always seem to attack us?" Anna asked.

I answered by shrugging my shoulders.

"Especially you, Viviana. It is so obvious that you guys can't stand each other. What happened between you two? Why is she so bitter with you?"

Anna was earnestly searching for information that I

wasn't willing to share. I avoided answering her questions directly and said, "She's just a bitter girl."

"She wasn't always so bitter," Anna pointed out.

"No, she wasn't." I had a vague memory of a time when Maya and I were inseparable.

Anna got out of the bed and retrieved her iPad. She powered it up and said, "How many of these educational apps have you downloaded?"

"Just a few," I answered.

"So, what's the real deal with you and Misalo?" Anna inquired.

"He's nice. He listens to me. I've never dated a guy who actually did that. Most of the guys I've dated were too busy trying to feel me up," I confessed as I thought about a boy I used to be close to named Frankie.

"Is that it? I mean, are you guys officially a couple? Have you officially taken him away from Maya?" Anna asked some tough questions.

"We've kissed and we like talking to each other. He hasn't officially asked me to be his girlfriend, but I think we're well on our way to being a hot couple. Do we look good together?" I asked cautiously.

"You guys look cute," Anna answered as she began touching the tablet's screen. "Look at this." She showed me a photo of a runway model.

"Who is that?" I asked

"I don't know, but I really like the designer outfit she's wearing. Don't you think it would look awesome on me?" Anna asked.

"Of course it would," I said, agreeing with her.

"I've been thinking about getting into modeling again," Anna said.

"I think you should," I agreed.

"I'm going to talk to my mom about it."

"Well, one thing is for sure, you certainly have what it takes," I said.

Anna shut down her iPad and lowered her head. Then she suddenly burst into tears.

"What's wrong?" I asked. I sat next to her and hugged her.

"I hate it when my dad yells at me. I don't like it when he gets mad at me."

I gave Anna a tight squeeze. I didn't know what to say, so I just held on to her and rocked her until she released all the hurt feelings she was trying to control.

Anna and I were interrupted by a knock at the door. When I glanced up, Maya was standing in the doorway.

"What do you want?" I snarled at her like a blood-hound from hell.

"I came to apologize to Anna," Maya said.

"Go away, Maya. I don't want to see you." Anna reached for a pillow and wrapped her arms around it.

"For what it's worth, I'm really sorry," Maya said and then remained silent. I think she was waiting for Anna to accept her apology, but Anna said nothing.

"Aren't you going to apologize to me, too?" I asked.

"Yeah, right," Maya said unsympathetically before she turned her back and walked away.

"Just ignore her," I heard Anna mumble.

"Yeah," I agreed. "I'm going to sit out in the backyard. Do you want to come?"

"No. I want to be alone right now," Anna said as she rested on her back and stared blankly at the ceiling.

Without saying anything more, I headed out.

When I got out to the backyard, Aunt Raven was bent over, vacuuming the inside of her car with a Shop-Vac from the garage. When she saw me walk past, she turned it off.

"Viviana, would you help me with this?" she asked.

I turned around and walked over to the passenger side of the car and opened the door. Aunt Raven was directly in front of me, removing the floor mats from the driver's side.

"Sure. What do you need?" I asked.

"Toss out all the empty cups for me," she said. I began gathering the old coffee cups.

"Why doesn't Uncle Herman clean out your car for you?" I asked.

"He usually does clean mine for me when he washes his, but I've decided not to wait until he decides to tidy up his vehicle again," she explained.

"Oh, okay," I said.

"Viviana, I know that you and Maya don't exactly see eye to eye, and I have a good idea why."

I froze when Aunt Raven said that. I met her gaze and couldn't bring myself to look away. I was transfixed, and there was nothing I could do about it. I finally found my voice.

"Huh?"

"I think you're angry, and you have every right to be. However, the person you're truly angry at is the one you love the most." Aunt Raven's words cut into me emotionally. I wasn't ready to have a deep conversation with her, nor did I want to.

I played dumb. "I don't know what you're talking about."

"Let me put it to you like this. When you deal with the devil, he sells you all types of lies and fills your heart with anger and deceit. The devil will cloud your mind with falsehoods and cause you to fight the wrong people."

"I still don't know what you're talking about," I said, breaking eye contact with her.

"You've put on a mask and you're trying to hide from me, but I see you, Viviana."

"You're confusing me," I said, wanting to move away from her. I didn't like the fact that she was playing with my mind.

"Did you know that when you were born, I was the only member of the family in the delivery room? Your father was out running the streets, and Grandmother Esmeralda was stuck in traffic. I remember your birth as if it happened yesterday. Once you were placed in your mother's arms, I stood beside her and opened up your hand with my pinkie finger." Aunt Raven held up her hand and wiggled her pinkie finger. "You clutched my pinkie finger, opened your eyes and looked directly at me. I saw you, Viviana. I saw all of your innocence and purity. When I look at you now, I still see it, but it is buried behind so many masks. You're afraid to let anyone get close to you and see you for who you truly are. Your heart is broken and has become corrupt with deceit."

I didn't know what to say, so I remained silent. I really didn't want to hear anything more that she had to say, so I forced my mind to think about something else and completely tuned her out.

Although my eyes were looking at Aunt Raven, I was seeing right through her. I was focusing on a memory that had surfaced from someplace very deep within a chamber of my mind.

The memory was of an incident that had happened a few days before my thirteenth birthday. I was with my dad and two of his friends from the neighborhood, Aurelio and Caesar. I remembered they were all wearing red bandannas. My father had given me his red bandanna to put on, and I remembered that I could smell the scent of the Head & Shoulders shampoo he used. It was summertime, and the sun had just gone down. He and his friends took me to Lawrence's Fisheries, which was located in Chinatown.

Lawrence's Fisheries was known for its deep-fried shrimp, which I loved. My dad bought an order that was large enough for us to share. We walked out of the restaurant to the parking lot, where the car we'd driven in was parked. I hopped onto the trunk of the vehicle, and my dad positioned the greasy brown bag of shrimp next to me, near my hip. I remembered ripping open the bag and grabbing two jumbo shrimp and biting into one. I didn't realize the shrimp was too hot, and as a result, I burned the roof of my mouth. I opened my mouth as wide as the sky and spit the food out.

"Damn it!" I cried.

My dad snapped his fingers and made Caesar run inside for a cup of ice. When Caesar returned, my father said, "Here. Suck on this ice cube. It will make the sting go away."

I did what my dad said and continued to whimper.

"*You have to be careful, Vivi. If the food has steam coming off of it, you have to wait until it cools off a little.*"

"*I know. I was just so hungry. You haven't brought me over here since I was a really little girl,*" I said as I sucked on the ice cube while reaching for another jumbo shrimp.

"*You said that you wanted to come here for your birthday, so I wanted to make sure I made that happen for you,*" he said as he reached for some food.

"*Hey, man, we've got trouble,*" said Caesar, who'd come over and slapped my father's back with the palm of his hand. Caesar nodded his head toward a car that had just pulled into the parking lot. The headlights were blinding and I had to hold my hand up and squint, but all I saw was the shadows of men getting out of the car.

"*Who are they, and why don't they turn off their headlights?*" I asked, thinking about how rude the men were.

"*Viviana, listen to me. I want you to get in the car. Lie down on the backseat, and don't look out the window.*" I could tell by the switch in the pitch in his voice that something was wrong.

Before I could ask any questions or even say, "*Okay,*" my dad pulled me down from the trunk, grabbed me by the wrist and hustled me into the backseat of the car. I positioned myself on my knees and looked out the back window. I had only a partial view because the trunk was now open. I saw my dad remove one of the baseball bats he played softball with and give it to Caesar, who was standing next to him. Vulgar and hostile words filled the air.

I then saw someone throw a punch at my dad. He avoided being hit by moving quickly. His fingers were curled into a powerful fist as he sized up his opponent, who threw another misguided punch. My dad maneuvered around the second punch *and quickly called on his skills as a prizefighter and released a series of quick snapping jabs. I heard the haunting sound of his knuckles smashing against flesh. Another man came up behind my dad, wielding an ice pick. He jabbed the weapon into my dad, and it made an eerie sound as it punched into the flesh of my dad's back. I screamed.*

"Daddy!" I tried to open the car door so I could help him, but when I reached for the door handle, Aurelio's face came smashing through the glass. I shrieked when I saw a large chuck of glass rip through the red bandanna and embed itself in his forehead. Aurelio's blood splattered on my nose, lips and forehead.

I curled up into a fetal position and prayed to God to make them stop. I heard the wail of police sirens and realized my prayers had been answered. I crawled out from behind the seat and took another look out the rear window. I saw Caesar helping my dad back to the car. I quickly moved over to make room for him as I saw Aurelio jump into the passenger seat with his hand pressed against his bloody forehead. My dad sat next to me, rested his head against the window and told Caesar to drive away quickly.

"You're hurt." I was frozen with fear and horrified by the amount of blood that was on my dad's clothes.

"Stop crying, Viviana. It's not as bad as it looks. I'm tough, and right now I need you to be a tough girl, too. I protected you from the bad guys. I wasn't going to let them hurt you," he whispered and then groaned.

"Why would they want to hurt me?" I tried not to cry, but I couldn't help it.

"Because they know how much you mean to me," he answered as he struggled to breathe.

"Please don't die, Daddy." I hugged him as tightly as I could, not caring about the scent of blood wafting in the air.

"I'm not going to die. It's going to take more than an ice pick to kill me. Don't worry, Viviana. We'll come back another day to celebrate your birthday. I promise we'll have fun," he said.

"I don't want any more shrimp from this place," I said tearfully.

"I told you we shouldn't have crossed the line and come over here," Aurelio said as he continued to apply pressure to the gash in his forehead.

"Don't worry, amigo. There will be retribution for this. No one ruins my little Viviana's birthday celebration and gets away with it," my dad said.

"I need to get to a hospital," Aurelio said.

"No. We'll go back to my place. Salena will stitch us up. She's very good," said my dad.

"Viviana, do you understand what I'm saying to you?" I could suddenly hear my aunt Raven's voice again. I'd tuned her out so well that she had to ask me if I was listening to her.

"Yeah, I hear you," I lied.

"Well, I hope so, because this little rivalry between you and Maya is ugly and I don't like it. It needs to stop."

"Sure," I said, just to satisfy her and get her to leave me alone.

"Do I have your word that you, Maya and Anna will do your best to get along? I know that it isn't easy for you to adjust to your mother being gone, but I hope that what I've told you about her relationship with your dad has helped."

"My dad?" I said. I truly had no idea what she'd just said about him.

"Yes, your father was a very complex man. He was very jealous and overprotective," she said.

"He was jealous because my mom was so beautiful, and I always felt safe when he was around. He never let anything happen to me or my mom," I said, defending his memory and his relationship with my mother.

"Is that what you believe? Is that what your mom told you?" asked Aunt Raven.

"It's the truth," I answered conclusively.

Aunt Raven sighed and then massaged the back of her neck. "I wish I could make you understand just how crazy things got between your parents," she said.

"It's not complicated to me. They loved each other and me. And then it all changed. It didn't have to, but it did. My mom hasn't been the same since he passed away and neither have I. I really hate—" I stopped talking before I said something I couldn't take back.

"Viviana, your anger and deceitful ways, combined with your stubbornness, are a perfect recipe for heartache, disaster and pain. I pray that all three don't happen at the same time."

"What are you talking about?" I was truly confused. It was then that I realized that tuning her out wasn't such a good idea.

"I'm going to be blunt with you, and I hope that what I say gets through your thick skull. Your mess is going to catch up with you and bite you on the ass, and when it does, it's going to hurt and the bite is going to be deep. Life took several bites out of your father's ass, but no matter how much life ripped him up, he never learned a single lesson. He kept doing the same thing and expecting different results. Don't be like him, Viviana. You have the potential to be so much more."

"My daddy was the best father a girl like me could've ever hoped for. I am proud to be his little girl, and I know that he'd want me to be just like him. Tough and fearless!"

"There is nothing wrong with being a strong woman, Viviana. Just don't be a dumb one," Aunt Raven stated.

"Are you calling me dumb?" My feelings were hurt.

"No, sweetie." Aunt Raven maneuvered around the car and came over to me. She placed her hands on my shoulders and said, "There is strength in you. I can see that, but there is also bitterness, and if you don't let your resentment go, it will destroy you."

Eighteen

MAYA

"Are you sure it's cool for me to be over here while your folks are at work?" Keysha asked as I shut the front door behind her when she walked in. Keysha was wearing a pair of denim slim-fit shorts and a white top. Her hair was pulled back off her face and tied into a cute ponytail. I, on the other hand, looked like a bum. I had on pink pajama shorts with a matching pink top. My hair was rather messy, but I wasn't trying to impress anyone at the moment.

"No, because technically, I'm still grounded for cursing out Anna at the dinner table, but I really don't care," I said as Keysha and I headed for the family room in the basement.

I sat in my dad's chair and Keysha sat on the sofa. I'd called her up because I knew that it was her day off from working as a lifeguard at the community pool. It wouldn't be much longer before the pool shut down for the season and she and I would be heading back to school. Anna, Viviana and my brother, Paul, were all at the pool, enjoying the few remaining nice warm days. Since they were gone, I wouldn't have to worry about any of them snitching on me.

"I thought you said Anna was grounded, as well?" Keysha said.

"Yeah, but since I technically started it, she got off a little easier," I admitted with resentment.

Keysha and I planned to just hang out all day and watch television. It was about the only thing we could do since I was under parental house arrest.

"I brought over a movie," Keysha said as she reached into her bag.

"Really? Anything good?" I asked excitedly.

"Have you seen the movie *Bridesmaids?*" Keysha asked.

"No, I haven't. What's it about?" I asked.

"Oh, my God! This is, like, the most hilarious movie ever. It's about two best friends who've known each other since they were kids, and one of them has found true love and is about to get married, while the other one is still. waiting for Mr. Perfect to come into her life," Keysha said "Grandmother Katie, Barbara and I watched it the other night. We had a girls' night in and ordered pizza while Mike and my dad were out at a Bulls basketball game."

"Why didn't you invite me over? I would have loved to hang out with you guys," I griped.

"I'm sorry. I didn't think to call you." Keysha placed a frown on her face.

"You're not sorry," I said teasingly.

"You're right," Keysha confirmed and then laughed.

Taking one of the cushions from the chair, I flung it at Keysha and said, "You could've just continued to lie to me."

"Why bother with lying? The truth is so much more liberating." Keysha laughed. "Anyway, this is, like, the best chick flick ever. We're going to laugh so hard our stomachs are going to ache." Keysha found the DVD in her bag and gave it to me. I placed the disk in the player and stood in front of the television with the remote in my hand, waiting for it to load.

"Do you have any microwave popcorn?" Keysha asked.

"Yeah, we should. I'll go check." I walked into the kitchen and found several packs of popcorn. I placed a bag in the microwave and stepped away. Before long, I heard Keysha yell out from the basement.

"Don't burn the popcorn, Maya. I can't stand the smell of burnt popcorn."

"I got this. I'm practically an expert at popping this stuff," I said, looking at the microwave to check the popcorn's status. Three minutes later I returned to the family room with the butter-flavored popcorn. The delicious scent was floating through the air, and I couldn't wait to dig in.

"Come sit next to me," Keysha said, patting the spot next to her.

"This had better be funny, Keysha," I said.

"Trust me on this one," she said just as the movie began.

Keysha was right. The movie was so funny that I nearly peed on myself from laughing so hard. After the movie concluded, I felt like baking brownies.

"Wow, I can't tell you the last time I had a brownie," Keysha said as she followed me into the kitchen.

"You're going to love my brownies. I use an old family recipe," I said confidently as Keyhsa sat at the kitchen table.

"What's the recipe?" Keysha asked.

"Well, if I told you, I'd have to kill you." I laughed.

"Ha-ha," Keysha said. "No, seriously. I'd like to make some at home."

Moving over to the refrigerator, I removed a magnet note pad and pen. I handed them to Keysha. "Here. Write down what I say," I instructed her.

"This is the formula for the best triple-layer brownies you'll ever eat. I use a large stoneware bar pan that's fifteen and a half inches by ten inches. Preheat the oven to three hundred fifty degrees. The first layer has one cup of creamy peanut butter. It also has one and a half cups of oatmeal—Quaker—a half cup of brown sugar, a third cup of all-purpose flour, a quarter teaspoon of baking soda, and a half stick of melted butter. Mix the ingredients together and press the dough into the pan as the crust. Bake it for eight to ten minutes. Now for the second layer."

"Hang on. Let me write that last part down," Keysha said.

"Okay. Let me know when you're ready."

"Okay, go," Keysha said.

"For the second layer, while the first layer is baking, prepare the brownie mix according to the package directions. I use two boxes of brownie mix. Remove the first layer from the oven and top it with the brownie mix. Spread the brownie mix all the way to the edges, and bake it for twenty-eight to thirty minutes, or until it's done. Then let it cool."

"Okay, I got that part. How do you do the third layer?" Keysha asked.

"Okay, for the third layer, you have to use one cup of semisweet chocolate chips and a half cup of peanut butter. Melt the chocolate chips in the microwave in a large microwave-proof measuring cup for ten seconds at a time, stirring until its smooth. Add the peanut butter and stir until it's well blended. Finally, top the brownies with the third layer and spread it all the way to the edges and let it cool."

"Damn, that does sound good," Keysha admitted.

"It is, especially with some ice cream," I said.

"Girl, what are you trying to do? Make me fat?" Keysha asked.

"No, just get you strung out on brownies." Keysha and I both laughed. "Put the pen and pad down and come over here and I'll walk you through how to make the brownies."

Keysha and I made the brownies as planned. The batch came out perfectly. I removed some vanilla ice cream from the freezer and placed a scoop on top of each of our brownies. Keysha and I then sat at the table and dug in.

"OMG. This is so freaking good," Keysha blabbered.

"I told you," I said, enjoying the taste of the morsel that was in my mouth.

"Seriously, I'm going to make a batch when I get home," Keysha said, rising up and moving over to the patio door. She looked out at the driveway and remained silent.

"See anything interesting out there?" I asked.

"You ever wonder what you'll be like when you get older?" Keysha asked.

"Like how much older?" I asked.

"Let's say thirtysomething, like the characters in the movie were. What do you think we'll be like?" Keysha asked.

"Good question," I said, then paused in thought. "Well, I'll probably be married to a rich man and living in California somewhere."

"Do you think we'll still be friends?" Keysha asked.

"Of course we will. Why would you ask a question like that?"

"It was just a random thought," Keysha admitted.

"What do you think your life will be like at thirty?" I asked.

"Well, since I don't ever plan on having children, I'll probably be a career woman. An attorney perhaps. I think I'd be a good lawyer."

"I can see that," I told her.

"What about you? Are you just going to marry rich and live happily ever after?" Keysha asked.

"No, I'd have to have my own career, as well. Probably something in politics. Now that Misalo wants nothing more to do with me, I've given up on the idea of marrying him, settling down and having babies."

"I know that I'm starting to sound like a skipping CD, but—"

I interrupted her. "No, Keysha, he still hasn't come clean about the pictures, but the jerk is officially dating Viviana, like you said."

"That sucks!" Keysha turned and faced me. "I figured

that something was going on, but I didn't think Viviana would actually go behind your back like that," Keysha said.

"Well, she did, and there isn't much I can do about it. As far as I'm concerned, Viviana is a total sleaze."

"What about Carlo? Have you been able to talk him out of fighting?" Keysha asked.

"No. He has his mind focused on beating up Misalo."

"I heard they've actually set a date, time and place," Keysha said as she sat back down.

"Are you serious? Carlo didn't mention that to me," I said.

"Does Geico sell insurance?" Keysha asked sarcastically. "I'm surprised he didn't say anything to you."

"I have to do something," I said aloud.

"Like what?" Keysha asked.

"Stop them from doing this," I answered, raising my voice. "Misalo doesn't know how to fight, and Carlo does. He's going to hurt Misalo."

"So, you're going to try to talk Carlo out of it again?" Keysha asked.

"Yes," I said, feeling a migraine headache developing.

"What are you going to tell Carlo?" Keysha asked.

"I don't know, but I'll think of something."

Later that day, after Keysha was summoned home by her dad, I called Carlo to try to talk some sense into him, but I couldn't get through. I sent him a text message and asked that he call me, because it was important that I speak with him. After I sent the text message, I found myself in the family room, watching an episode of *Lincoln Heights*. Viviana came into the room through the garage entrance. She glanced at me, but we didn't say a word to each other. A few minutes later, she came back through the family room and was about to head out the door again.

"Where are you going?" I asked, breaking the silence between us.

"Someplace that you can't," Viviana mocked.

"It's almost dinnertime, and you know how my mother likes for everyone to be home so we can sit together and eat," I reminded her.

"I won't be gone that long." Viviana turned to walk out but then stopped. She turned back around and said, "If you must know, I'm going to see Misalo."

I glanced at her. I felt the animosity I had for her heating up.

"He's such a great kisser," Viviana added, continuing to taunt me. "That's why I have to teach him how to fight. I wouldn't want him to get those sweet lips of his split open."

My stomach turned at the thought of Misalo kissing her. "What do you mean, teach him how to fight?" I asked.

"Just what I said. I've been teaching him how to throw punches and combinations. Just like my father taught me. Don't you remember how well I kicked your butt?"

"Go to hell, Viviana!"

"You first, trick!" she roared before turning her back on me and continuing on.

When Carlo finally got back to me, there was still enough time for me to sneak out of the house and meet with him face-to-face. I told him to meet me at the park, which was only a block away from my house. I arrived there first and sat on the park bench and listened to music I'd downloaded on my iPod. After a few songs played, I looked at my watch to check the time.

"Dang it, Carlo," I said aloud. "My parents will be home in thirty minutes." I phoned Carlo again to find out where he was. I didn't get an answer. I waited for another fifteen minutes and then decided that I'd better get back home before I got busted for sneaking out of the house while being grounded.

As I walked down the sidewalk toward my house, Carlo came creeping along the street in his car. He blew his horn, rolled down the passenger window and said, "I wasn't that late, was I?"

Frustrated, I stopped, turned toward Carlo, who was leaning over while looking at me, and said, "I don't have time for games, Carlo. I told you that I needed to see you right away and that it was very important."

"I got here as fast as I could, Maya. What more do you want?" he asked.

"You could've called and told me where you were and how long you'd be. Why didn't you answer my call fifteen minutes ago?" I asked.

"It's against the law to be on the phone while driving." He smiled at me. I knew he was attempting to win me over. "Come on. Get in so we can talk about your issue." He waved for me to join him. I huffed as I opened the passenger door and sat beside him.

"I don't have very much time, Carlo. I told you that I

was grounded, and now I have less than ten minutes to get back to the house."

"Well, then, you'd better speak fast. What's up?" he asked. There was no easy way to ask him not to fight Misalo, so I didn't waste any of my precious time beating around the bush.

"I don't want you to fight Misalo," I said.

Laughing, Carlo said, "That's not going to happen."

"Really? You're not going to fight him?" I asked, holding my breath and awaiting confirmation.

"Oh, no. We're going to fight. We're going to throw down tomorrow," he said proudly.

"What's the big deal? Why can't both of you just let this male ego thing go?" I wanted realistic answers, but I didn't know if Carlo was capable of providing them.

"Look, Misalo is a cocky jackass who needs to be put in his place. He needs to be taught a lesson about sticking his nose in my business," Carlo replied, raising his voice at me. I could tell by the look in his eyes that his resolve to hurt Misalo was unwavering.

"Please," I begged him.

"Don't you realize that I'm also doing this for you, Maya? Have you forgotten that?" Carlo asked.

"Yes, and I appreciate that, but I don't want to see you get hurt," I said.

"Please. I can beat Misalo down with one arm tied behind my back. This isn't going to be a long fight," he said confidently. "Trust me. By the time I'm done with him, he not only is going to apologize to me, but I'm going to make him say he's sorry to you, as well."

Finally, giving in to the fact that I wasn't going to

change his mind, I asked, "Where are you guys supposed to be fighting?"

"Veterans Park. Tomorrow at noon. There are going to be a lot of people there. Everyone knows about this fight. I can't wait to publicly humiliate Misalo." Carlo smacked the closed fist of his right hand into the palm of his left.

"Oh, damn! I've got to go!" I said, urgently opening the car door.

"Do you want me to give you a ride back home? You'll get there a lot quicker," Carlo offered.

"No. They might see me in your car, and then I'd never hear the end of it," I said. I cut through the park and started running toward my house.

NINeteen

"Are you ready, baby?" I asked Misalo. I was at his house, helping him make final preparations for his big fight with Carlo. Misalo was standing in front of his bathroom mirror, shadowboxing.

"Jab, jab, hook, uppercut," he said aloud as he practiced maneuvering.

"You've gotten better." I was impressed with his hand speed.

"Yeah. I'm ready to take this fool down," Misalo said, firing off a series of quick punches.

"Save some for the fight, baby," I said as I approached him from behind and gently placed my hands on his shoulders. I massaged the back of his neck, which he rotated counterclockwise. "Remember, don't let him get you on the ground. The boxing skills I showed you won't be of much help if you're on your back," I reminded him as he put on a black tank top.

"He's not going to take me down. I'll introduce his face to my knee if he tries to go for my legs." Misalo was talking tough. I could see the contempt he had for Carlo in his eyes. "Let's do this," he said, looking at himself one more time before walking out.

I followed behind him and said, "I've got your back, baby."

"I know you do, Viviana." Misalo paused and briefly kissed me. When our lips met, I swear time felt as if it stopped. His lips were so soft and, as far as I was concerned, tasted delicious.

"Do you think Carlo will show up?" I asked once I snapped out of my brief moment of bliss. I picked up the first-aid kit I had decided to purchase just as a precaution. If Misalo got hurt, I wanted to make sure that I'd be able to handle patching him up, just like my mother had patched up my father.

"That punk had better show up. If not, I'm going to go hunt him down," Misalo said as he and I walked out his front door.

When we arrived at Veterans Park, a crowd of people was waiting on Misalo to arrive. I didn't know how so many people had found out about the brawl They were anxiously waiting for the mayhem to begin.

"I was beginning to think he was a coward," I heard someone say as Misalo and I walked toward an open area of the park where there was plenty of space to fight.

"He's not afraid," I snapped at the person who had the audacity to think otherwise.

"I hope this will be a good fight," I heard someone else say.

"What are they fighting about?" asked someone else in the crowd.

Misalo and I finally stopped walking when we saw

Carlo. He was standing with his shirt off, flexing his muscles. A few other guys were standing beside Carlo. Since they looked alike, I assumed they were either his brothers or cousins. Carlo was clearly more muscular than Misalo, not that Misalo looked wimpy. Carlo just had a body that appeared to be chiseled out of stone. He had strong shoulders, a mighty chest and a well-defined six-pack. The black tank top Misalo was wearing made his biceps look strong, but I feared that if he took a solid hit from Carlo, the fight would be over and Misalo and his pride would be wounded for a long time.

I had thought for sure that Maya would be standing next to Carlo, but she wasn't. I searched around the crowd and spotted her standing next to Keysha. I thought that it was odd for her not to stand by Carlo's side, since he was clearly her new man. Maya caught my gaze, and we looked at each other for a long moment. I could see fear and uncertainty in her eyes. I knew that this was something she had hoped would never happen, but there was nothing she could do to stop it. The fight was going to go down. I decided to remove my cell phone and take a few snapshots of her to use against her. Her girlfriend Keysha noticed me taking photos. She was glaring at me, as if I were a difficult mathematical problem she was trying to figure out how to solve.

"Where are your friends?" I whispered to Misalo after I put my camera away. I feared that if he started winning, Carlo's sidekicks would get involved in the brawl, which would mean that I'd have to help out, and I did not want to fight a guy.

"I don't know. The guys from the soccer team are supposed to be here," Misalo whispered as he looked around for his boys. He spotted them making their way through the crowd. "Here they come," he said, nodding his head in the direction from which they were approaching.

I gave a sigh of relief. Four of Misalo's soccer friends showed up to support him. If things got out of hand, at least the odds were now even.

Misalo took off his tank top and flung it to the ground, signaling he was ready to throw down.

"Are you ready to get beat down, boy?" Carlo roared as he stepped closer to Misalo with his hands balled up, eager to do bodily damage.

"You're the one who is about to get his butt kicked!" Misalo barked back.

"Come on. Let's do this!" Carlo shouted as he closed the gap between himself and Misalo.

I tried to get Misalo's attention to remind him to protect himself and not to get caught up in the moment by throwing wild punches.

"You're going to learn not to get in my business, punk!" Carlo said aggressively, making gestures with his hands and arms.

"And I'm going to teach you a lesson about messing around with another guy's girl!" Misalo fearlessly growled back.

"You shouldn't have sent those private photos of Maya to all the contacts in your cell phone. That was bogus, man. Maya dropped your punk ass because she wanted to get with a real man who respected her and wouldn't disrespect her!"

"I never sent the photos out of my phone. What the

hell are you talking about?" Misalo momentarily looked perplexed.

"What? Now you're going to say something lame, like you lost your phone?" Carlo continued to antagonize Misalo.

By the bewildered look in Misalo's eyes, I could tell that he wasn't concentrating on winning the fight.

"Misalo, if you never sent the photos, then who did?" I heard Maya ask.

"Who cares, baby! Can I get a picture of you with all your clothes off?" some dude behind me yelled out. I turned and looked at him. He was a tall, skinny kid with brown freckles and a bad haircut. He was showing some friends of his the photos in his phone. "Do you want to see that Maya chick in her underwear, too?" He flipped his phone around so that I could see Maya's photos that had been forwarded to him.

I could've cared less. At that moment, I heard the crowd explode with a loud roar. I turned back around and saw that the fight had begun.

"Get him, Carlo!" I heard someone shout out as Carlo inched closer to Misalo, who was looking for the perfect opportunity to throw a punch.

"Move!" said a girl who was standing near me. She had her cell phone in her hand and was recording the action. I took a quick glance around and noticed that practically everyone who had a cell phone was recording the fight.

The moment Carlo got close enough, Misalo swung at him but missed.

"If you're going to throw a punch, you'd better learn how to connect!" Carlo taunted Misalo.

"Come on, Misalo!" I called, cheering him on as the mob grew impatient. Carlo once again moved in closer. Misalo allowed him to get too close, and Carlo unleashed several quick blows to Misalo's ribs. Misalo was able to push him off. Carlo charged back in and Misalo caught him with a solid shot on the jaw.

"Yeah! Yeah! Yeah!" the flash mob of teens screamed, as if they were watching their favorite performer at a concert.

Carlo absorbed the strike. Misalo swung several more times but missed.

"Take your time, Misalo!" I shouted.

"You are truly a punk. You have to have your girl yell out instructions to you," Carlo said, moving in once again.

Maya finally said something. "Both of you, just stop!"

Her request fell on deaf ears. Carlo charged in once again. Misalo tried to hit him but missed. Carlo swept Misalo's legs out from under him and got him on his back.

"Get up!" I shouted as the crowd circled around the two of them so they could watch Carlo pound his fists into Misalo's skull. It didn't take long for Carlo to let his fists fly. Misalo was taking a beating, and the crowd loved it.

"Carlo, that's enough!" Maya rushed in and jumped on Carlo's back, pulling him off of Misalo. The crowd jeered Maya for breaking up the action. Maya released Carlo and tumbled out of the way. Misalo quickly got to his feet and rushed toward Carlo. Misalo now had Carlo in the same position and returned the favor with a series of hammer fists.

"Kick his ass, baby!" I yelled, cheering Misalo on.

That's when the fight got dirty. One of Carlo's cousins joined in and kicked Misalo off of Carlo. Misalo tumbled over. The odds weren't even. There were four guys beating up on Misalo. I immediately jumped into the action and kicked one of the guys off. Misalo's friends then joined in. Everything suddenly turned chaotic. There was screaming and shouting. The mob seemed to have taken on a life of its own. It was like a living, breathing mass of violence.

It didn't take long for the fight to turn into an all-out brawl. People who had just been watching were all of a sudden caught up in the madness and punching. Some girl decided to hit me for no reason. I defended myself and hit her with a four-punch combination that knocked her flat on her ass. The next thing I knew, her girlfriends appeared out of nowhere to help her beat me down. Before they could make a move, I nailed two of them, one with a roundhouse punch and the other one with an uppercut punch. The crowd had gone haywire. People were screaming and shouting.

The swarm of people moved like a cyclone toward a nearby creek. I followed it because I needed to find Misalo. I needed to know if he was okay. Several people fell into the creek, Maya included. She looked as if she'd fallen pretty hard, but I didn't care about her. I heard the wail of police sirens. As the authorities drew near, the mob scattered and ran in multiple directions. I saw Misalo limping away briskly with the help of Maya's friend Keysha. I chased after them for what seemed like forever. They finally stopped in front of a church that was down the street from the park. They sat down on the lawn. By the time I caught up to them, Keysha was having a very serious conversation with Misalo.

"I want a straight answer from you, Misalo," Keysha said, not caring about the fact that Misalo was clearly injured. His nose was bloody, his bottom lip was bleeding, there was a cut in his eyebrow and his ankle was swelling up.

"A straight answer about what?" Misalo winced as he tried to rotate his left foot in a clockwise motion. "I think I twisted my ankle."

"Let me look at it," I said, squatting down. It was then that I realized that during the commotion, I'd lost the first-aid kit.

"Why did you forward all the photos that Maya took for you? Those pictures were like a special gift from her to you. Why did you play her like that?" I didn't like the fact that Keysha was questioning Misalo.

I rudely tried to get rid of her. "Why don't you just leave? I'll take care of him." I made certain that my tone of voice wasn't a pleasant one.

Keysha ignored my suggestion, as if I were an unwelcome ant at a picnic.

"Carlo said the same thing. I never forwarded those photos!" Misalo said.

"Are you happy now? Just leave, Keysha, so I can help him!" I gave her a second warning.

Reaching into her small purse for her cell phone, Keysha said, "Yes, you did, Misalo, and here is proof. See, here is the text you sent, along with the date and time."

"Why would you keep a photo of your girlfriend like

that? Do you have a crush on Maya or something?" I interjected, trying to switch the focus of the conversation by suggesting that she and Maya were secret lovers.

"Maya is my best friend, which is something you lack," Keysha retorted. "Besides, I did delete the photos. I didn't realize that I still needed to delete them from the trash folder on my phone." Keysha forced Misalo to focus on what she was showing him. "Look at the images and the date and time, Misalo."

"Wait a minute. That was the day I broke up with Maya at the pool. I didn't send these pictures. I never would have sent them," he said.

"Look, chick. You've worn out your welcome," I said, rising up and approaching Keysha. "Now leave!" I threatened her.

Keysha issued her own warning. "I don't know who you think you're talking to, but you'd better get out of my face!"

"Leave!" I shoved Keysha, who backed up a few steps. Keysha was not afraid of me at all. She quickly returned the favor and shoved me back.

"If you put your hands on me again, I'll kill you!" Keysha looked me directly in the eyes.

"Would you two be quiet! I'm trying to think. Is this what Maya has been trying to talk to me about?"

"Duh! You're just now figuring that one out?" Keysha asked, reaching into her purse. She removed some tissue and said, "Take care of that bloody nose."

"I can take care of him!" I snapped at Keysha. I wanted her to leave.

"You can't take care of a pile of crap sitting in fresh

toilet water!" Keysha shouted, insulting me, and I didn't like it one bit. My blood was starting to boil, and I was only a hair trigger away from beating Keysha down.

"How did these photos get forwarded?" Misalo was totally confused, and the last thing I needed or wanted him to do was figure out what happened.

"Forget it, baby. She's talking crazy. Maya probably sent her over here to spy on us," I said, not wanting Misalo to do something stupid, like actually think.

"Yeah, right. I've got better things to do," Keysha said but didn't stop asking questions. "Why didn't you delete the photos like Maya had asked you to?"

"Because the pictures were so beautiful, I just couldn't bring myself to delete them," Misalo solemnly admitted.

"Oh, give me a break! Maya isn't all that. I'm prettier than her, aren't I?" I snapped at Misalo for being such a sap.

"You wish you were half as good-looking as Maya!" retorted Keysha, insulting me again, and I wasn't going to take that from her.

"That's it!" I said and shoved her. Keysha shoved me back and grabbed my hair, and I reached up and grabbed a handful of hers.

"Would you guys stop! Keysha. Let her hair go. You, too, Viviana. Let Keysha's hair go." Misalo immediately broke us apart.

"You're not so tough!" Keysha said as she spat. I noticed that her saliva was red with blood. I figured she had accidentally bitten down too hard on her bottom lip.

"I'm not broken. You didn't break me!" I snarled at her as I touched the area on my head where she'd grabbed my hair. It was very tender. When I looked at the pads of my fingers, I noticed blood.

"Yes, I did!" Keysha insisted. That was when I noticed her flicking a patch of my hair from her fingers. She'd actually ripped it from my skull.

"Why don't you stay out of my damn business!" I screamed as I looked for another perfect opportunity to attack her. I wasn't done with her just yet.

"It was you!" Misalo pointed his finger at me.

I took my focus off of Keysha and glared at him. I thought he'd at least be concerned about my missing hair, but he was too busy having an epiphany to notice.

"What are you talking about, Misalo?" Keysha asked, spitting on the ground once again.

"Viviana, you had my phone after you showed me the video clip of Maya slow dancing with Carlo at that party. Don't you remember? I got so upset about the video clip that I rushed into the swimming pool and broke up with Maya. When I came out, you said that I dropped my phone, and returned it to me." Misalo had a look of betrayal in his eyes. He'd finally put the pieces all together.

"You did that, Viviana? To your own cousin? What kind of sick heifer are you?" Keysha glared at me as if I were a pile of steaming horse manure.

"I don't know what you guys are talking about!" I said, denying Misalo's allegations. I was so focused on Misalo and the betrayal in his eyes that I didn't notice Keysha, who'd heard more than enough of the allegations to make her own judgment.

"How could you do that to your own cousin?" Keysha asked again, searching for a reasonable explanation.

In my anger, I inadvertently admitted to something. I said, "Because she deserved it! That's why!"

"Why?" Misalo hollered, so intensely that I flinched with fear. The roar of his emotional pain was unnerving. "You're the cause of all of this? My breaking up with Maya, the fights with Carlo, everything! You set Maya up, didn't you?"

"It's not like that. You don't understand everything she's done to me. Don't judge me until you know the full story. I don't regret a damn thing!" I said unapologetically.

"I hope you rot in hell, Viviana!" Keysha said as she moved away from us.

Now that Keysha was gone, I could do damage control with Misalo. "Baby, just forget I said that. Let me help you." I tried to tend to his injuries.

"Get away from me, Viviana. We're through!" Misalo's words cut me deeply.

"You don't mean that. I know you don't. You're just angry right now, and I can understand that, but you shouldn't be," I said, then paused in thought as I tried to think of a reason for him to forget everything.

"Viviana, I don't want to see you anymore," he said and began hobbling back toward Veterans Park, to where he'd parked his car.

"How can you say that? How can you just turn your feelings for me off like that? I know you don't mean it, baby. I know you love me, Misalo," I screamed, but Misalo didn't acknowledge me. He continued on his way. I stood still, trying to decide if I should follow him or leave him alone.

Then I heard someone shout out, "There she is!"

twenty

MAYA

when I got home, I went directly into my bathroom and removed my wet clothes. I had to take my time and peel off my jeans, because I'd busted my left knee and the blood had soaked through the fabric, causing it to stick to my skin. I couldn't believe I'd gotten pulled into a free-for-all. One minute I was pulling Carlo off of Misalo, and the next thing I knew, all hell had broken loose. People were pushing and punching each other for no reason.

Some strange girl, who I'd never met or seen before, slapped me and said, "That's for sending those nasty photos of yourself to my boyfriend!" I'd had enough of people mortifying me about the photos. Why Misalo hadn't heard about the photos and stood up for me, I didn't know. All I did know at that moment was that I wasn't taking it anymore. I shoved the girl so hard that she tumbled into another girl and fell to the ground. Figuring I'd made my point, I searched the crowd for Keysha, not knowing that a tidal wave of people, screaming and fighting, was about to swallow me whole.

Before I could move out of the path of the rowdy flash mob, I was pulled into it. I literally had to fight my way out of it. I was being kicked and punched from every direction. It was like being at a concert where a brawl had broken out, and there was no way I could get out of the path of danger. I scuffled my way through the mayhem and was shoved into a thicket of trees and bushes near the edge of the creek. I slipped on the muddy embankment and tumbled downward through undergrowth, which ripped and scraped my skin, before finally splashing into the creek and crashing my knee into a rock that was beneath the surface. I clawed my way up the muddy embankment and inadvertently sliced open the heel of my hand on a jagged tree branch. Once I made it onto the grass, I heard the wail of police sirens. I quickly searched for Keysha but didn't see her. There was no way I was going to stick around to answer the questions the police would have, so I gathered myself as best I could and hobbled home.

Once my jeans were totally off, I cleaned my knee up, which had begun to swell. My knee was bruised pretty badly, and it was throbbing. I took a shower and washed my hair so that I'd no longer smell like swamp water. Afterward, I bandaged up my knee and my hand and went into my bedroom and found a pair of shorts and a clean T-shirt. I knew I needed to put ice on my knee to help the swelling go down. I hobbled down the stairs and over to the kitchen. I located the ice pack my mom kept in the freezer for my brother, Paul, who was always doing something stupid that required an ice pack. Once I had what I needed, I maneuvered my way down the few steps that led to the basement. I sat on the sofa, elevated my leg and rested the ice pack against my knee.

"Damn, that's cold," I complained as I leaned my head

back and rested it against a sofa cushion. No sooner had I exhaled a sigh of relief and closed my eyes than my cell phone rang. I saw that it was Keysha calling me.

I quickly answered the phone. I was praying that Keysha was okay and hadn't gotten hurt. "Hello?"

"Where are you at?" Keysha asked. I could tell by the edginess of her voice that something was wrong.

"I'm at home," I said as I adjusted the ice pack. "You didn't get caught up in that brawl, did you?" I asked.

"No, but I did get into a scuffle with Viviana," Keysha admitted.

"With who?" I was uncertain if I'd heard her correctly.

"I'll tell you later. Right now, I really need you to come over to my house," Keysha said.

"I can't. My leg is messed up," I griped.

"Your leg is messed up? What happened to you?" Keysha asked.

"It's nothing too serious. I just fell into the creek," I explained.

"Can you walk? You didn't break your leg again, did you?" I could tell that Keysha was legitimately concerned about me.

"I'm not hurt that badly," I said.

"Maya, I really need you to come over. I wouldn't ask if it wasn't serious," Keysha insisted.

"Why don't you come over here?" I suggested.

"That isn't a good idea right now, trust me," Keysha said. After pausing for a brief moment to think about the quickest route to Keysha's house, I said, "Okay. Give me fifteen minutes and I'll be there."

"Great. I'll be waiting," Keysha said and hung up the phone.

★ ★ ★

I rode my bike over to Keysha's house. I figured it would be easier than hobbling all the way over there on one leg. For the most part, it was easy, but for most of the way, I had to pedal with one leg while I dangled the injured one. Keysha's brother, Mike, opened the door for me.

"Hey, Mike," I greeted as I stepped inside.

"What's up with you, girl? Why did you try to stop the fight when Misalo was getting his butt kicked?" he asked. Mike was wearing a pair of Levi's jeans and a Ralph Lauren polo shirt.

"Because I'd seen enough," I answered as I maneuvered around him.

"I don't know if I would've protected him after what he did," Mike said.

"Most people wouldn't. In spite of everything, I still didn't want to see him get hurt." I paused for a moment. "How are you and Sabrina getting along?"

"We'd get along much better if she'd learn her position and stay in her lane."

"What?" I looked at him as if he were stupid.

"Sabrina just needs to understand that girls other than her find me attractive. I can't help the fact that I'm so fine and irresistible." He laughed at his conceited comment. "I mean, why is it that girls freak out if they see their guy talking to another chick?" he asked, searching for a concrete answer to his question.

Shrugging my shoulders, I said, "It depends on the girl and how secure she feels."

"What exactly does that mean?" he asked as I held on

to the rail and hobbled up the stairs and into the family room.

"It means that you have to let her know constantly that she's number one and that you're not interested in other girls," I said.

"I can tell her that all day long, but it doesn't help. I just don't get that. How could she possibly justify getting angry with me just because some other chick thinks I'm all that?"

"Women are complicated, Mike," I said as I made my way toward Keysha's room. Once I made it to the top landing, I saw Keysha standing in her bathroom. When she turned to face me, I saw her pressing a towel against her lip.

I hobbled over to her as quickly as I could. "What happened?" I asked.

"That's what I'd like to know from you," Keysha said.

"Me? What are you talking about?" I said as I sat down on the edge of her tub. "And is your mouth bleeding? Did you get into another fight?"

"I got into a fracas with Viviana over you and bit down on my tongue too hard," Keysha said as she turned to face me. She reached over and closed the bathroom door so we'd have privacy.

"Viviana!" I said, utterly shocked.

"Yes," Keysha answered.

"But why?" I asked.

"Because I was talking to Misalo and I asked him straight up why he'd sent photos of you to all his contacts."

"Are you serious? What did he say?" I was on edge waiting for her next words.

"He denied it. He said that he never sent the photos," Keysha said.

"How could he possibly deny doing that? He was the only person I sent the pictures to," I said, getting angry.

"He acted as if it was the first time he'd ever heard of it," Keysha said.

"Well, I don't see how. All his friends should've gotten copies. Hell, they've been sending me all kinds of perverted emails, telling me how they'd love to do me."

"Maybe no one told him because they liked the photos. Who knows?" Keysha said. "Are you still getting wild messages from guys?"

"Hell, yeah. I just don't say anything. I feel like there's this big sign on my forehead that says, 'Maya is a total freak. Come give her a try.'" I released a depressing sigh. "Misalo was my soul mate. I just don't understand what happened to us."

"Viviana is what happened to you guys," Keysha said as she closed the lid on the toilet and sat down.

"Yeah, I know that already," I said, hoping that she had more current news.

"No, you don't. There is more to it than her just stealing him away from you. She's the one who caused the breakup to begin with," Keysha explained.

I sat very still. "I'm listening."

"Misalo blasted you out at the swimming pool that day because Viviana showed him a video clip of you dancing with Carlo the night she left you at that party."

"What!" I shouted at Keysha.

"You heard me," Keysha said.

"That witch must have stood around long enough to take a video clip of me dancing with Carlo. Slow dancing with him was the only way I could get him to give me a ride home," I explained.

"Well, when she showed it to Misalo, she must've made up some story about you guys being a hot item," Keysha said.

"That's what caused Misalo to go over the edge. Ooh, I'm going to kill her." I was fuming and wanted revenge.

"Wait, that's not everything," Keysha replied.

"What else is there?" I asked.

"When Viviana had Misalo's phone, she went through it and forwarded the pictures. Misalo never deleted them because, he said, you looked too beautiful."

My mouth opened as wide as the horizon "He lied to me. He said that he deleted them."

"Well, you already knew that he lied about that, but you should've never sent them to him to begin with."

"What did you just say to me?" I was offended.

"I'm just saying. I'm your best friend, and I'm saying you should've never sent them."

"Well, I had my reasons for doing it," I said, not wanting to admit fault.

"I don't need to hear about your reasons. That's between you and Misalo. What I want to know is, why does Viviana hate you so much?"

I met Keysha's gaze, and I supposed the look in my eyes told her that I was carrying a very big secret.

"Come on. I have a right to know. This is the second fray I've gotten into for you with Viviana."

"It's complicated, Keysha," I said as I shifted my focus toward the ceiling.

"Yeah, I can see that," Keysha said as she reached over and took my hands into her own. "I'm your best friend. You can tell me. Your secret is safe with me," Keysha assured me.

I thought about whether or not I should tell her. Part of me wanted to, but another part was very hesitant.

"Come on. It's okay," Keysha said, trying to coax the truth out of me.

I finally gave in and told her what the deal was. "It's about Viviana's father. He was a hoodlum and a well-known gangbanger. He was the *corona* of the Latin Kings in Chicago back in the early nineties."

"What's *corona*? Is that like the beer?" Keysha asked.

"No. *Corona* means 'crown.' Get it? Like a king wears a crown?"

"Got it," Keysha said. "Go on."

"Anyway, he pretty much stayed in his own neighborhood and didn't venture outside of it very much. When Viviana turned thirteen, he took her out for a birthday dinner in another gang's territory. There was a big gang fight, and Viviana watched everything as it went down. She even saw a guy get his face smashed through a glass window. Anyway, her dad was badly injured when all was said and done. Viviana freaked out because she thought he was going to die. When he got well, he went and found the rival gang member who stabbed him with an ice pick. He beat the guy so badly that he died. Someone snitched on her dad, and the next thing the family knew was the police were looking for her dad, who was

hiding out with my aunt Salena at my grandmother Esmeralda's house.

"At the time, I was spending my summer there, along
with Viviana. Anyway, one night I couldn't sleep, so at
about three in the morning I got up and was planning
on watching television in my grandmother's living room.
As I was coming down the stairs from the second floor,
I saw Viviana's father standing at the front door, talking
to a member of the Latin Kings who had come to give
him information. I overheard her father give out orders
and name some people who were to be dealt with. I even
heard him brag about how he'd beat and killed the man
who stabbed him. He even said the guy's name. Neither
Viviana's father nor the other gang member knew I was
listening to their every word. They frightened me, so I
went back into the bedroom with my grandmother. The
next day, my mom came to pick me up after I pleaded
with her. I told her that I didn't want to stay with Grandmother Esmeralda anymore. I told her that I was scared.
My mom wanted to get to the bottom of what had happened, but I didn't want to say anything."

"Did Viviana's dad do anything to you?" Grandmother Esmeralda asked.

I said, "No."

"He frightens you, doesn't he?" asked Grandmother Esmeralda.

"Who frightens her?" asked Viviana, who'd just walked in
on the conversation that I was having with my grandmother and
my mom.

My mom said, "Viviana, go into the other room with your
mother."

"My mom made Viviana leave. Viviana didn't go far. She stood in the hallway and eavesdropped on our conversation. From my point of view, I could see her standing still and listening to our every word."

"Mom, I told you not to allow Salena to stay here with her boyfriend," said my mom to Grandmother Esmeralda.

"What was I supposed to do? They had no place to go. Besides, he was only supposed to stay for a few days, and he left this morning."

"Grandmother Esmeralda argued with my mom. In the middle of their fussing, there was a loud knock on the front door. My grandmother went to answer it, and Viviana followed her. The next thing I knew, four cops walked into the kitchen, where my mom and I were. They began asking questions about Viviana's father. They wanted to know if he was there."

My mother asked, "Why are you looking for him?"

"We're doing a death investigation and we need to ask him some questions," answered one of the officers.

"My mother and grandmother remained quiet. They had no idea what he'd done, but I knew."

"So, did you tell the police?" Keysha asked.

"No. They left, but they gave my mother and grandmother a card and said to call them if they found out any information on his whereabouts."

"Well, how did the cops even know to come to your grandmother's house to search for him?" Keysha asked.

"Who knows? Maybe someone tipped them off, or perhaps the cops followed him there. Either way, someone talked, and snitching was something that could get a person killed."

"Okay, but that doesn't explain why Viviana hates you so much," Keysha said.

I exhaled deeply before I continued. "My mom and Grandmother Esmeralda continued to argue. My mom was concerned about Grandmother Esmeralda's safety. She feared that gangbangers would come to the house and attack her. Viviana, who had wandered out of the room to watch the police leave, came back into the kitchen and said, 'Don't worry. My dad is tough and everyone fears him. He'll protect everyone.'"

"Your father is a mean man," I said. "He hurt someone, and I heard him telling it to someone who came here in the middle of the night, while everyone was asleep."

"Everyone got quiet after I made my little secret known."

My mother then asked, "Is that why you called me and told me you were afraid? Because of what you overheard?"

Fearfully, I answered, "Yes."

"What did you hear?" asked my mom.

"I laid it all out for her, and when I was done, Grandmother Esmeralda did one of the hardest things ever. She forced my aunt Salena to tell her where Viviana's dad was and then tipped off the police. They picked up Viviana's dad and brought him in for questioning. As it turned out, several eyewitnesses pointed him out in a lineup and he was detained. They eventually matched blood samples from the victim's body to Viviana's father, and off to prison he went. He was locked up for about a month before he was killed. It was retribution from a rival gang. After his death, Viviana blamed me. She said that had I kept my mouth shut, her father would be alive.

I felt guilty about that for a long time. At one point, I even had to go to therapy for it." I looked up at Keysha and her face had turned pale. I hadn't talked about the animosity between Viviana and me in a very long time.

Keysha finally broke the silence. "I see why she hates you so much."

"Do you think I deserve what she's done to me?" I swallowed hard as I waited to hear Keysha's thoughts on the matter. I was certain she was going to say that yes, Viviana's hatred for me was fully justified and that I didn't deserve any kind of happiness.

"I believe that you did the right thing. It sounds like the guy was kind of creepy, and I know that I would have been afraid, as well, if I overheard him say he killed someone."

I exhaled a sigh of relief. "I'm so glad that you don't think I'm a bad person," I said, moving next to Keysha and draping my arm around her. I gave her a tight squeeze. At that moment my cell phone rang.

"Who is that?" Keysha asked.

"Believe it or not, it's Viviana," I said, wondering if I should answer it.

"Answer it. At least now you can tell her that you know what she's done," Keysha insisted. Keysha was right. I needed to confront Viviana about her evil ways. I was about to get really nasty with her.

"Hello," I answered, with venom in my voice.

"Maya! Oh, my God! Oh, my God! I don't know what to do." Viviana sounded hysterical and forced me to pause for a moment. I'd never heard her sound so unhinged.

"Viviana, what's going on?" I asked, sensing something had gone very wrong.

"I need your help, Maya!" Her breathing was labored.

"Are you running or something?" I asked.

"Yes. A gang of girls is chasing me. They said that they know that I was the instigator of everything that went down with Misalo and Carlo."

"Well, you are," I said unsympathetically. In the back of my mind I was hoping she'd get beaten down.

"Please, Maya. I need your help. I can't fight them all off. I'm around the corner from the house, cutting through the park." I heard Viviana release a murderous shrill. Then the call dropped.

★ ★ ★ ★ ★

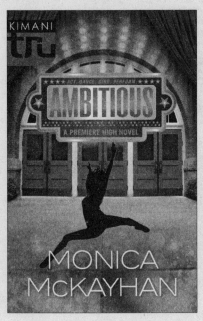